Fire and Rain

Rain Mystery Trilogy Book 3

David Homick

Fire and Rain

Copyright © 2022 David Homick

All rights reserved.

Published by Blue Knight Media

The characters, incidents and dialogs in this book are fictional and are not to be construed as real. Any resemblance to actual events or persons, living or dead, is completely coincidental.

"I've seen fire and I've seen rain."

James Taylor

Chapter One

An unexpected knock on your door when you live in the middle of nowhere is never a good thing.

I eased the door open, and my back stiffened. "I thought I told you never to come back here."

Three months ago, on Thanksgiving Day, a stranger named Finn Rafferty showed up at my front door claiming to be Jenn's husband. I felt like a fool, standing there with an engagement ring burning a hole in my pocket. Jenn and I had lived together for seven months on the ranch she inherited from her uncle, and I had finally worked up the nerve to pop the question in front of family and friends.

"May I come in?" He hugged himself against the cold.

I folded my arms. "You can try, but I wouldn't recommend it."

His eyes shifted back and forth. "Is Jennifer home?"

It bothered me he was back asking for Jenn. It had been three months since I threw him off our porch. Where has he been? Why was he back now? And how do we keep him away for good?

"She's not here." I shifted my weight. "What's your play?"

"My play?"

"What are you after?" I took a step forward to intimidate him. It worked. "You show up here after all this time, claiming to be Jenn's husband. What do you think is going to happen?"

"Sounds like you don't believe me." He pulled a folded paper from his back pocket and held it out between us.

I slapped it out of his hand. "Jenn is *my* girl, and no piece of paper from you or anyone else is going to change that."

"That's a legal document." He picked it up and took a deep breath. "You may have bullied your way through life, but it isn't going to change the fact that the State of Kansas recognizes us as man and wife."

"You're not in Kansas anymore, Dorothy."

He pulled a second paper from his pocket and set them both on one of the porch chairs.

"Jenn says the marriage was annulled. It's like it never happened. So, I suggest you leave now and never come back."

"And what if I don't?"

"You can leave in that car... or in a body bag. Your choice."

One side of his mouth turned up to form a crooked smile. He walked down the steps. I followed.

Jenn and Alex walked out of the stables and stopped when they saw me talking to Finn. Jenn said something to Alex and sent him back inside. She looked madder than a wet hen as she marched toward us.

"There she is," Finn said as the crooked smile made another appearance. He waved in her direction like he wasn't here to destroy our lives.

I stepped into her path and held up my hands. She responded with a *get-out-of-my-way* glare, and I obliged.

"What are you doing here?" she huffed.

Finn looked around deliberately. "I like what you've done with our ranch."

Jenn's face reddened, and I felt the heat coming off her. She folded her arms across her chest. "Our marriage was annulled. You have no claim to anything here."

"Apparently, he didn't get the memo," I said.

"I don't have to move into the main house, just yet. One of those cabins down by the river will work for now. I might even help with chores."

"We don't need any help."

His eyes narrowed. "We'll see about that."

It sounded like a threat. I'd heard enough. "Finn was just leaving." I stepped between the two and puffed up my chest. I got up in his grille. "Wasn't he?"

Finn hesitated, but I left him only one option. "I guess I was." He relaxed the muscles that had tightened in his neck.

I took a half step forward, and he retreated.

Jenn stood at my side as we watched him walk toward his car. I made a mental note of the license plate.

"I'll be in town for a while. We should have coffee, get caught up." He climbed into his car.

"Yeah, that's not gonna happen," Jenn responded. "Y'all better not come around here again."

He waved out the window as he spun his tires and kicked up gravel on his way down the drive.

Jenn flipped him off with both hands.

"Did you ever bring him here?" I asked. "You know, back in the day?"

She looked about ready to give me the same two-finger salute Finn just got. "Never."

"How did he know about the cabins?"

"I don't know." She paused, then turned and walked away.

I called after her. "We need to talk."

"That's all we've been doing." She turned and looked at me as she walked backward. "I'm getting tired of it. I guess y'all better decide who you believe—him or me." She turned and headed off toward the stables.

"So that's it?"

"I need to get Alex, then make dinner," she said without looking back.

Jenn had adopted Alex, an eleven-year-old boy whom I'd rescued in Afghanistan before Jenn and I met. He'd ended up in an Army hospital in Germany where Jenn had been stationed, and the two became friends. When Jenn returned stateside, she searched for him and made arrangements to take the boy that no one else wanted.

Imagine my surprise when I arrived in Colorado to find the boy with the war-torn soul living with my girlfriend. Jenn took him in and gave him a second chance. He called me GI Joe back then. I never knew his name. Jenn decided that Pop was a more appropriate moniker, probably hoping that we would become a family someday.

Jenn was scared and pissed at Finn or maybe herself. I didn't know which. I thought I'd been doing a good job of being patient with her. Jenn wasn't the only victim here. I could lose everything. She'd been reluctant to talk about her past, but that would have to change. It didn't look like Finn Rafferty was leaving any time soon, so I had to find out more about him and whether there was any truth to his claims.

I sat on the step feeling queasy and out of sorts, much like I did after a PTSD episode. The air was warm for the end of February, but a cool wind blew under my jacket and sent a chill down my back. I pulled up my collar.

The memories I'd tried to bury from my tour in Afghanistan were resurrected from time to time after I returned stateside, usually triggered by a loud noise or stressful situation. Plenty of both had been available in my hometown of Bradley, Texas.

I hadn't had an episode since I moved to this ranch in Middle-of-Nowhere, Colorado.

One thing that helped me relax was a unique blend of herbal tea made for me by a Cherokee medicine woman named Leotie just before she died. Mama had convinced me to see her, and I reluctantly agreed. She had deep-set onyx eyes that could see into my soul. She knew things about me no one could have possibly known and made the tea specifically for me from herbs she picked herself. I called it rain dance tea because of a dream I once had. She passed away last year, so I can't get any more. I'd been rationing it, but I might need a cup tonight.

I took a few deep breaths, my head in my hands. When I looked up, I saw Jenn and Alex approaching.

"Dillon, you look like hell. Are you okay?"

I shook my head. "Not really."

"Did you have one of your flashbacks?"

"No." I wiped the beads of cold sweat from my forehead with the back of my hand. "I reckon I had one of yours."

CHAPTER TWO

I didn't like what Finn's return was doing to our relationship. Jenn didn't talk much about her past, and I didn't press her. The past was past. We were here, and we were solid. If Finn hadn't darkened our doorstep last Thanksgiving, we would surely be planning our wedding.

I couldn't propose to a married woman. As implausible as Finn's claim was, it shook me, and I was keeping the ring in my pocket until I could sort things out. I probably should have sat them both down and settled it once and for all, but my temper got the best of me. I'd thrown him off our porch with a warning to never return.

Jenn admitted they had been married shortly after she enlisted, but she'd had it annulled before she shipped out overseas and hadn't seen or heard from him since. She had no idea how he had found her, or why he would show up now with such an outrageous claim.

They'd had a whirlwind romance that ended in a small civil ceremony. But Finn Rafferty was a grifter, a small-time con artist who lied to her and treated her poorly after the wedding. Being young and naïve isn't a crime, but the way he treated her should have been.

We thought we'd scared him off, that he'd given up and moved on to find another mark. Now he was back with papers and the notion that he might move in. According to Jenn, if Finn's mouth was moving, he was lying. The papers he'd left were a copy of the marriage certificate and a screenshot showing that the Leavenworth County Court Clerk had no record of their annulment on file. I knew about the first. The second troubled me.

Jenn put Alex to bed and returned downstairs. She saw me sitting in the living room and made a quick turn into the kitchen.

"Not so fast," I called.

"What?"

She knew what. "We need to put an end to this Finn thing before I do something we might both regret." I patted the cushion next to me on the sofa.

She crossed her arms after she sat, a classic defensive posture.

"Tell me I'm not living with a married woman."

"Dillon, we've been over this. We were married for a short time, but I had it annulled."

"The Leavenworth County Clerk doesn't agree."

"What are you talking about?"

I handed her one of the papers Finn left on our porch.

"What's this?"

"You tell me."

She studied it. "Where'd you get this? Have you been checking up on me?"

I shook my head. "Finn gave it to me."

"And you're just showing me now?"

"That's not the point. Finn seems to think you're still married. Why would he think that?"

"I don't know. Everything is legit. I have a copy of the judge's decree." She huffed. "Do I need to show it to you?"

"I believe you…"

"It sounds like you don't."

"Something doesn't add up."

She stood. "Maybe y'all should sleep on the couch tonight, me being a married woman and all."

"C'mon, Jenn. I'm on your side."

"How come it doesn't feel that way?"

I watched her walk back up the stairs.

She had a stubborn streak, alright, but so did I. I wasn't going down without a fight.

I grabbed a coat and a bottle of Jim Beam and headed for the stables. I needed to talk to someone who wouldn't give me an attitude. Chance had always fit that description.

The temperature had reached nearly 60 degrees that afternoon, unusually warm for the end of February. The thick blanket of snow that covered the ground only a week ago was all but gone. Chance saw me coming and was quick to let me know he approved of my impromptu visit. The cool night air had made its way inside the stables, so I grabbed one of the extra horse blankets in case my visit turned into a sleepover.

I shoved a couple of bales of hay together across from his stall and took a load off, setting the bottle down next to me. Chance snorted and shook his head like he knew why I was there.

"Don't you start, too," I said. "I thought this was a no judgment zone."

I took the first of many hits off that bottle. I had to stay warm, right?

"In case you hadn't heard, there's a new guy in town," I said. "And he's fixin' to cut me out of the picture. But don't worry, boy, I won't let that happen. I'm counting on you to have my back."

Chance whinnied and nodded like he understood every word I said.

After all, I had his back last year when the ranch was under attack and the horses were poisoned in the pasture. Two of the horses didn't make it. Jenn and I worked with the vet to save the others. We stayed all night in the pasture with Chance and Remington to monitor their recovery.

"I don't know what to do. If Finn had some kind of accident and ended up dead, that would solve all of our problems, wouldn't it? I'm not saying I could do something like that myself, but I might be able to hire the Whitehawk brothers." I waved a dismissing hand at Chance like it was his idea. "Nah. It's still too early in the game to be thinking like that."

Jenn seemed confident that Finn's claims were baseless. He seemed just as confident that they were legit. Was he bluffing? That would be pretty stupid. Something like that should be easy enough to prove. You'd probably have to hire a lawyer, but...

I stood. "Chance, ol' boy, you're a genius. I'll call Mort in the morning and have him look into it. He can answer the question once and for all, and he'll know what to do if things go sideways."

Mort Anderson had been Daddy's close friend and attorney back in Texas. I used him for advice and counsel, not to mention he was presently Mama's significant other. In fact, he was here with Mama for Thanksgiving when Finn made his first appearance. He'd never let me down, and I was sure he wouldn't want to start now.

After another half hour of discussing my options, I began feeling the effects of Mr. Beam. Chance looked like he wanted to get some shut-eye, as well. I screwed the top on the bottle, pulled the blanket over me, and drifted off to sleep.

CHAPTER THREE

The ground shook beneath me, and I crossed back over the borderline of sleep.

"Wake up, Sunshine," Buck said as he kicked one of my hay bales.

I looked up through squinted eyes to find Charlie "Buck" Owens standing over me. The sound of hungry horses filled the air.

"What are you doing?" I asked as I pulled the blanket off and sat up.

"Morning chores. You remember chores, don't you?"

"It's morning?"

His laugh sounded like truck tires on a gravel road. "That must have been a real barn burner."

"What?"

"That fight you had with the missus last night."

"It wasn't a fight."

Buck had been the ranch foreman for longer than even *he* could remember. I heard he came with the ranch when Jenn's Uncle Roy bought it back in the '70s. We almost lost him last year when an explosion rocked the barn. I was supposed to be in there with him, so I don't know which one of us was the intended target, but I reckon it was supposed to be a two-fer.

He once told me that, "There ain't a leaf that blows 'round here that I don't know about. That's just bein' a good foreman." That might be what nearly got him killed back then, but right now, it was just what I needed.

"I have a favor to ask," I said.

Buck eyed me suspiciously as he spat a stream of tobacco juice from under his bushy gray mustache. I'd never asked him for anything before. In fact, I don't like asking favors of anyone. I learned at an early age to fend for myself.

He pulled the top from a round tobacco tin and put a pinch inside his cheek. He held the open tin up to my face. "Want a pinch?"

It smelled like horse shit with a touch of mint. "I'm good."

Buck hooked his thumbs in the pockets of his overalls. "What can I do you for?"

"A guy named Finn Rafferty was here yesterday. Did you happen to see him?"

He nodded.

"Good. If you ever see him on the ranch again, I want to know about it."

"Who is he?"

"Remember last Thanksgiving when a guy knocked on our door and sent the rest of the day into the toilet?"

"Kinda hard to forget."

"Finn was that guy."

"What's he doing back here now?"

"That's what I want to know. He claims he's married to Jenn. Even showed me papers."

"So they're hitched?"

"The jury's still out on that one. But Jenn told me he's so crooked he has to unscrew his britches at night."

"Poor girl. What can I do?"

"I reckon we haven't seen the last of his sorry ass. I need you to keep your eyes peeled. If you see him snooping around here, you have my permission to get rid of him anyway you see fit. Right now, he's public enemy number one."

Buck smiled and let another stream of tobacco juice fly. "Count me in."

"Good. Also, let me know if you see him in town or learn where he's staying. He's probably renting a place, or maybe has a motel room here in town. And he's driving a brown Honda, plate number Alpha Bravo X-ray 3-8-6."

"Is that all?" His overgrown mustache curled up at the ends and I nearly saw his upper lip. "What color Jockeys was he wearin'?"

"This is serious, Buck."

"Sorry." His mustache fell back into place and his brow furrowed. "By the way, that other fella come by here again askin' for Jenn."

"What fella?"

"The one that won't take no for an answer."

"Someone else has been looking for Jenn? What's his name?"

He reached into the front pocket of his overalls, produced a business card, and handed it to me. "He left this."

Jameson Crowley from Riverdale Gaming.

"I told him we ain't sellin'."

"He wanted to buy the ranch?" I said, still looking at the card.

"Said he'd pay top dollar."

Neither of us said anything as I rubbed the rest of the sleep from my eyes. I stood and slipped the card into my back pocket.

Buck finally broke the silence. "Seein' as you set me back a good half hour, how about you help me feed and water the horses?"

***

After helping Buck with the horses, I returned to a somber mood inside the house. Jenn glared at me when I walked in, and Alex knew enough to look for something to do in another room.

"Y'all look one wheel down and the axle dragging," she said. "Did you sleep with the horses?"

I ran my hands back through my hair, and a few pieces of hay fluttered to the floor. I brushed them aside with my boot. "They're good company."

Her expression told me she took my comment the way it was intended. "Well, I hope y'all had breakfast with 'em, 'cause this kitchen's closed."

"I'm not hungry." I lied. "Maybe you can show me those annulment papers now."

She put her hands on her hips. "You really don't believe me, do you?"

"Of course I believe you. I wouldn't ask to see them if I didn't think you had them."

She frowned as she considered my explanation. My home-grown logic worked, and she headed for the stairs. She returned with papers that she held in front of my face with both hands.

"Now, we're making some progress." I snatched them from her.

I scanned two pages of legal jargon. On the second page, I read: NOW THEREFORE, IT IS HEREBY ORDERED that the marriage of Plaintiff and Defendant is declared null and void and of no effect, and each of the parties is restored to the status of an unmarried person.

"Well, counselor?"

I handed them back to her. "Looks legit to me. Maybe we should let Mort take a look at it. He should be able to tell us what's what."

"Knock yourself out."

"Great, but before I call, is there anything else he should know?"

"Like what?"

"I don't know… Any other husbands, do you have any kids, were you ever abducted by aliens?"

"Call him if that'll make you happy, but don't be a jackass."

"I'd like to settle this Finn thing once and for all. I thought you would feel the same."

"I settled it a long time ago and moved on. Finn is dead to me."

"News flash, Babe. Finn Rafferty is very much alive, and I have a bad feeling about why he suddenly showed up in Redfield."

"Okay, call him, already."

"I will. But first," I removed the card from my pocket and gave it to Jenn. "You know anything about this?"

"Looks like a business card."

"Can't get anything past you." She may have been trying to diffuse the situation with humor, but I wasn't in the mood. "I meant, ever heard of that guy, or Riverdale?"

"Where'd you get this?"

"Buck. Said he's been coming around looking for you. Said he wants to buy the ranch."

She took another look at it. "Riverdale owns a few casinos out west."

"Sounds like they're fixin' to move to Colorado and build another one on your land."

"Maybe y'all should call Mort." She handed the card back, her eyes shrouded in fear. "I think I know why Finn's back."

I wasted no time getting Mort on the line and explaining the situation. He couldn't tell me much without reviewing the documents, so I let him go with the understanding that I would fax him the papers and he would follow up with me on Monday.

We didn't have a fax machine, so I drove down to Hattie's Hardware to use hers. Hattie and me, we hit it off the first time I walked through her door. She was an easygoing, ex-hippie who smoked a joint now and then. She'd been to Woodstock in 1969; drove there with Buck and a few friends, but that's a whole other story.

A tiny bell jingled and the smell of leather, fertilizer, and fresh-cut lumber met me at the door. Hattie looked up from behind the counter. She wore her usual denim apron over a red flannel shirt with the sleeves rolled up. Her long gray hair had been pulled back behind her head, but a few wayward strands that broke free framed her kind face. Fiery eyes hinted that she'd been a force to reckon with back in her day.

She waved me over, all eight of her bracelets jangling. "Dillon Bishop. If you aren't a sight for sore eyes. Get over here and give Hattie a big hug." I noticed she often referred to herself in the third person.

I obliged. I guess I hadn't been around for a while. Winter had hit the area hard between Christmas and the middle of February, and the whole town hunkered down. It occurred to me I hadn't seen her since Thanksgiving, and I apologized for not making more of an effort. We'd had her family over for dinner at the ranch—her son Ziggy, a good friend and acting Teller County Sheriff, and her daughter Raven, who taught Alex at the public school.

"It's been too long," I said.

"And whose fault is that?" She raised an eyebrow above a smirk.

I raised my hands. "Guilty as charged."

"What ya got there?" she asked when she saw the papers in my hand.

"I need to send a fax. Number's right there on the first page."

Hattie gave it the once-over before feeding it into the machine. Her long turquoise earrings swung playfully as she shook her head. "Is this about last Thanksgiving?"

Being the county clerk, she made it a point to know everybody's business. I didn't mind.

"Sure is."

"You got a keeper there. You know that, right?"

I smiled and nodded before I let my expression fall. "You know anything about Riverdale Gaming?"

Chapter Four

I didn't sleep with the horses Saturday night, but I woke up alone Sunday morning. I found Jenn in the bathroom hugging the toilet.

"Looks like someone snuck out last night and tied one on."

She didn't appreciate my attempt at humor.

"Sorry. Are you alright?"

"I'm sick over this Finn thing. You don't know what he's capable of. He'll find a way to destroy me again."

"I'm not going to let that happen."

Jenn made Alex his favorite blueberry pancakes for breakfast, more out of guilt than anything else. Admittedly, we'd been neglecting him for more pressing matters.

He surprised us at the table with a loaded question. "Mama, are you and Pop getting a divorce?"

What did a little kid from Afghanistan know about divorce? I wanted to tell him that would be impossible because Jenn was married to somebody else. I bit my tongue.

Jenn put her hand on his. "Why would you ask that?"

"Because you're always fighting." He said it matter-of-factly, but I saw the fear in his eyes.

I thought we'd kept things pretty civil around him, but I've been told that kids can be very perceptive.

"No, honey. We're not getting a divorce."

At least she didn't have to lie to him.

"We're just trying to resolve some things about the ranch. They're important things, so sometimes we get a little upset. Y'all don't have to worry about it. Mama and Pop will figure it out together."

Good to know.

Alex pushed his plate away. "Can I be excused?"

Jenn and I nodded simultaneously, relieved that the Q & A session had ended quickly and on a somewhat positive note.

"That didn't go as badly as I expected," I said when he'd left the room.

"I don't feel well. I'm going to lie down."

"I'll get the dishes," I said as she walked up the stairs.

I put Alex's dishes in the sink and turned on the faucet. I guess I could have handled this Finn thing better, but it's not something I could have seen coming. It made me wonder how many more skeletons might be hanging in her closet.

I didn't like all the drama. I also didn't like the fact that this current episode was making her ill. Truth be told, I didn't feel so well myself.

On account of the weekend, I wouldn't hear from Mort for at least another twenty-four hours. I had to find a distraction.

I felt bad for what this was doing to Alex. He'd been through much worse in his short life, but this wasn't Afghanistan, and we'd vowed to give him a better life. This war was not his, and I would make damn sure he didn't end up as collateral damage again.

I found him in his bedroom playing video games.

"Put on some warm clothes. We're all going for a trail ride."

He looked up, confused. "Mama's going, too?"

"Of course. It was her idea." Sometimes you need to stretch the truth a little. "It's Sunday afternoon, the weather's clear, and it's about time we did something as a family."

He flashed a smiled so big I thought the top of his head might fall off.

I returned his smile, and we fist-bumped. "We leave in fifteen."

But first, I had to go break the news to Jenn that we were all going on a trail ride.

***

A pristine blanket of snow covered the ground and clung to the tree branches. Six inches had fallen the night before, and under the midday sun, the fields looked covered in diamonds. With Alex on Romeo, yours truly on Chance, and Jenn on a new mare named Dixie, we set out for Fletcher's Pond and points north.

At first, Jenn had balked at the idea of a family trail ride, claiming she felt sick to her stomach. A convenient excuse, I thought. I convinced her to suck it up and do this for Alex. He deserved better than the way we were behaving lately, and the underlying situation was likely to get worse before it got better. I reminded her we were on the same team, and we needed to unite against this common enemy.

She said it might be a good opportunity to get some riding time on Dixie, as well. Jenn had nursed the young mare back to health after rescuing her last month from an abusive situation at a nearby ranch. Poor Dixie was a mess when we got her, not unlike me when I returned from Afghanistan.

"You sure you want to ride Dixie? Maybe it's too soon."

Jenn dismissed me with a wave of her hand. "She'll be fine."

That horse seemed too skittish to be away from the paddock, but what do I know about training horses?

For nearly an hour, we moved at a leisurely pace, making small talk and even laughing from time to time. Jenn appeared to be feeling better, and Alex looked happy. I'd be lying if I said that things didn't feel close to normal.

I thought I saw something reflect the sun up ahead near a stand of Spruce. Before I could get a good look, it disappeared. I told myself it was nothing, but my bad foot tingled in my boot. A souvenir from halfway around the world.

I'd been riding in a Humvee with a little Afghan boy—Alex—in my lap. I'd found him sitting in a bombed-out building with his dead parents, so I'd grabbed him up and loaded him into our vehicle. When we hit an IED, I instinctively covered up the kid, but the blast took my boot and a couple of toes with it. Since then, I would get a tingling sensation in my foot when something bad was about to happen. Okay, the two might not be related, but more often than not, it held true.

I motioned the others to follow me and headed to where I'd seen the shiny object. We stopped when I noticed tracks along the pasture fence. I jumped down to check it out. Snowmobile tracks. They followed the fence line and disappeared into the trees.

We had a couple of old snowmobiles in one of the outbuildings, but as far as I knew, neither had been running in quite a while. Maybe Buck had brought one of them back to life and was riding the fences. Not likely. Who else would be out here? I couldn't shake the feeling that Finn might be back.

Jenn's horse bucked sideways, and she pulled hard on the reins to straighten her. Dixie snorted and threw her back in protest, but Jenn calmed her quickly. She spooked much easier than the other two. I wanted to say *I told you so*, but I kept my thoughts to myself.

I mounted up, and we followed the tracks, stopping when we reached the edge of the clearing. Several trails led into the woods, but I didn't think we should follow any of them today. When I turned to tell the others that we should think about heading back, an engine roared to life. A snowmobile shot out of the woods fifty feet in front of us.

The startled horses bucked. Chance reacted quickly to my attempts to regain control. Romeo was not as willing. I kept an eye on Jenn as I jumped down to help Alex. Dixie was in a full-on panic. Jenn pulled hard on one reign to get her back feet moving laterally so she couldn't rear up. I grabbed Romeo's reins to keep him on the ground. Then I held out a hand and pulled Alex off.

Panic washed over Jenn's face as she struggled to gain control. Dixie wouldn't respond to anything Jenn did to keep her on the ground. Jenn kicked her feet from the stirrups to try an emergency dismount, but Dixie reared up so high and hard that Jenn couldn't hold on. She fell to the ground and didn't move. If she was okay, she would have moved out of the way to keep from being trampled.

My first instinct was to run to her, but I knew I had to keep Dixie away. After warning Alex to stay back, I positioned myself between Jenn and the rearing horse. I started waving my arms and hollering to scare her away. I didn't want to make things worse, but I didn't know what else to do.

It worked. Dixie bolted. I bent down over Jenn. She didn't move. I said a silent prayer as I searched for a pulse. Weak, but still beating. I wanted to sit her up, try to rouse her, but I knew better. If she'd injured her neck or spine, which was all too likely, I could make thing much worse.

Alex approached in tears. "Is Mama okay?"

I turned and put my hands on his little shoulders. "Mama's going to be fine, but we need to get her help in a hurry."

"I want her to get up. Please help her."

"I want that too, but we can't move her until help arrives."

I pulled out my phone. No signal. "Stay with her while I call for help."

He stared at her lifeless body, and I imagined how difficult the memories were for him.

"Alex."

He turned to me, his bottom lip quivering.

"You can't touch her."

He nodded through tears.

I'd expected to lose cell signal, but not until we got past the pond. I jumped up and ran thirty yards into the clearing. *One bar.* I dialed 911.

Chapter Five

Alex and I watched helplessly as the medevac chopper lifted off and banked to the left, en route to Pikes Peak Regional Hospital in Woodland Park. The roar of the engine and the thumping of the rotor brought back unwanted memories. I put my arm around Alex's shoulders, sure that he was dealing with some memories of his own.

We hurried back to the ranch. Woodland Park is a twenty-five-minute drive from Redfield. I planned to make it in fifteen. Halfway back to the house, we met Buck coming the other way.

"What happened?" he called when he got within earshot.

"A snowmobile spooked the horses."

"A snowmobile? Up here?"

I nodded. "Jenn got thrown. She was still unresponsive when they airlifted her to the emergency department in Woodland Park."

Buck winced as the color drained from his face. "Sounds pretty bad. What can I do?"

"She was riding Dixie. I can't find that damn horse. Maybe you can collect her."

"That explains why I seen her outside the pen, all saddled up and no rider. When I heard the helicopter, I got a bad feelin', and I come out to see what's what."

"I need to get moving. I'm taking Alex with me to the hospital."

"Maybe he should stay here with me."

"No, he needs to be with his mother. I need *you* to keep an eye on things here. We need to find out who was on that snowmobile and what he was doing on our property."

I gave Chance a kick, and we took off for the ranch.

***

We made it to the emergency room in fourteen minutes. The nurse at the desk told me Jenn was being examined, and we would have to wait. The doctor would be out as soon as he was through. She handed me some paperwork to fill out while I waited. I did the best I could. It bothered me how little I knew about the woman I planned to spend the rest of my life with.

I hated waiting. Jenn's life might be on the line. I knew there was nothing I could do, but waiting made it worse. Alex asked a bunch of questions that I couldn't answer. I kept checking the time on my phone. Another two minutes had just passed. I wanted to call someone—Mama or maybe Hattie, but they would surely have more questions that I couldn't answer. I needed to wait until I heard from the doctor.

Alex sat quietly, rubbing his eyes from time to time. He appeared to be handling this better than me, as I paced around the waiting room. He loved sports, so I flipped through the channels on the TV, looking for something that might distract him. A replay of last year's World Series was in the fifth inning on ESPN Rewind. I turned to Alex with a raised brow, hoping for a nod, but all I got was a shrug. I left the game on and resumed pacing.

A half hour, which seemed like a half day, passed before a doctor wearing blue surgical scrubs entered the waiting room.

"Wait here," I said to Alex and walked over to the doctor.

"I have good news and bad news," he said after he pulled off his mask. "An MRI revealed cerebral edema. Her head trauma has caused her brain to swell. I started her on an IV steroid to control it. It's a relatively small amount at this point, but if it gets worse, it will require surgery to relieve the pressure. I'm a little concerned that she hasn't regained consciousness. We'll be monitoring that closely."

Let's hope that was the bad news. "You said there was good news?"

His facial muscles relaxed. "Yes. She has no broken bones... and there appears to be no harm to the baby."

I blinked back my surprise and confusion. "The baby?"

"Yes. Ms. Miles is three months pregnant."

I glanced at Alex, sitting patiently with his hands in his lap. "Are you sure?"

"We drew blood when she arrived. There's no doubt."

I had to process. How long had she known? Why had she kept it from me? Is that why she'd been feeling sick? I'd thought it was stress.

"I need to get back," the doctor said.

"Sure. Thank you." I was having trouble concentrating. "Uh... when can we see her?" I said as he walked away

He turned. "I'll let you know."

I returned to my seat next to Alex.

"Can we see Mama now?"

"Not yet. The doctor said it's best if we let her rest a while."

He hung his head.

I nudged his arm. "Let's go see if they have any ice cream in the cafeteria."

He shrugged.

I told the nurse where we were going, then returned to Alex. "C'mon, pardner." I waited for him.

We ran into Hattie in the hall on the way to the cafeteria. I was so distracted that I almost walked right past her.

"Dillon."

"Hattie? What are you doing here?"

"How is she?"

I gave my head a quick nod in Alex's direction. "Doctor says we need to let her rest before we can see her."

Hattie gave me a knowing look.

"We're headed to the cafeteria to get some ice cream. Why don't you come with us?"

After we found a table, I gave Alex a fiver and told him to go pick something out.

"Aren't you having any?"

"Not right now."

He turned to Hattie and waited. She shook her head.

I looked at Hattie after he left. "How did you hear?"

"Ziggy called. He overheard them dispatch the helicopter." She placed her hand on mine. "How is she?"

"She's still unconscious. She hit her head so hard that it caused her brain to swell. Doc said if they can't control it with drugs, she'll need surgery." I kept the pregnant part to myself. "Doctor's gonna let us know when we can see her."

A silence descended on the table.

"Where's Buck?" Hattie asked.

"I left him back at the ranch. I reckon he'll be by later."

"I wouldn't count on it."

I tilted my head. "Why not?"

"It's Sunday."

"He doesn't strike me as the church-going type."

"He's not." She smiled. "Every Sunday, he brings dinner to his friend Curly."

"Buck? I don't understand."

Hattie leaned forward, elbows on the table. "You might not know it, but Buck's got a big heart, and he's as loyal as the day is long. About three years ago, his closest friend, Curly Stenshorn, lost his wife of forty-one years when their house burned down. He never quite recovered. He lives alone and doesn't know much about takin' care of himself. That was his wife's job."

She paused, and I waited for her to continue.

"Ever since, Buck fixes Sunday dinner and delivers it to Curly. He usually brings a bottle of whiskey, and they make a day of it. I imagine that's where he'll be for the rest of the day."

"Buck's always working, but he takes Sundays off." I shook my head in disbelief. "I had no idea."

"Consider me here for the both of us. I'm sure he'll stop in tomorrow when Jenny's feeling up to visitors." She offered a hopeful smile. "In the meantime, if there's anything I can do…"

"You're doing it. Thanks for being here for us."

After a couple moments of silence, I did a little relationship recon. "It may be none of my business, but it seems like you and Buck have become an item."

"You're right." She smiled. "It *is* none of your business."

"I'm sorry."

"Don't be." Her smile widened. "Like I said, Buck has a big heart, and we have a lot of history."

Alex returned with a half-eaten ice cream bar and the first hint of a smile I'd seen since the accident. Hattie handed him a couple of napkins and pointed to his face.

Hattie's phone lit up and vibrated on the table. "Ziggy said he's on his way."

We waited for Alex to finish his ice cream, then headed back to the waiting room to find Hattie's daughter, Raven, there. Alex ran to her and gave her a big hug. Raven seemed more like a second mother to Alex than a teacher. I guess, technically, she would be his third.

Ziggy arrived a few minutes later, and I caught them both up on Jenn's condition while Hattie distracted Alex. Ziggy pulled me aside after the others had taken their seats.

"This is probably not the right time, but I was wondering if you've given any more thought to my offer."

"I did, but with Jenn down like this…"

"You can work part time. I really need the help."

"I've thought about it a lot, but like you said, it's not the right time. Wouldn't I have to go to school or something?"

"With your military record and firearms training, they'll waive the usual academy class. You'll have to study the procedure manual, but otherwise, you're in."

"Just like that?"

"I might have put your application in and told them it was an emergency."

"What emergency?"

"I can't do it all myself. I'm busier than a one-legged man at an ass-kickin' contest."

"I thought you had another deputy."

"Bill Connors. He's stationed in Cripple Creek and covers the south end of the county. Things have been heating up here with this casino thing and I have a feeling it's about to explode."

"Are you talking about Riverdale Gaming?"

He nodded. "Riverdale owns a bunch of casinos in three states and has its sights set on Teller County for a big resort—casino, hotels, even an airport. They bought up most of RMA's land at a fire sale after the attorney general shut them down. Now they're buying up property around Redfield from whoever they can convince to sell."

"I don't see how anybody would want that in their backyard. Who's selling?"

"The problem is, some locals want to sell, and the rest want to lynch them for even thinking about it."

"Could get messy."

"Exactly."

"A guy from Riverdale has been visiting the ranch looking for Jenn. Says he's willing to pay good money to buy the ranch."

"What's Jenn say?"

"I don't think she'd sell. She thinks Finn Rafferty might be involved somehow. He still claims to be married to Jenn. I've got a lawyer friend looking into it."

Ziggy looked me in the eye. "Can you do me a favor?"

"Maybe."

"Riverdale is holding another meeting tomorrow night for anyone interested in their proposal. I asked Bill to help me keep the peace. Maybe you can attend in an unofficial capacity. You know, get the lay of the land. I think things are going to get worse before they get better."

"Jenn's my first priority, but I'll see what I can do."

"Thanks." He leaned in closer. "So, what happened out there?"

"We were on a trail ride when I noticed snowmobile tracks near the north pasture, so we followed them, but lost them in the woods. Whoever it was must have seen us coming. When we got close, he made a run for it and spooked the horses. Jenn's horse threw her. She hasn't regained consciousness yet, and I'm getting worried."

"Snowmobile, huh? You're not the only one. I've had three other complaints in the last week."

"I figured it was Finn."

"Maybe on your land, but what about the others?"

"Jenn thinks he's mixed up in this Riverdale thing." I shook my head. "If I find out it was him, I'm gonna kill him." I fired off a couple of rapid blinks. "I guess I shouldn't be telling *you* that."

"You shouldn't be telling anyone that." He said it with the hint of a smile. "I ran the plate you gave me. It's a rental."

"Do you know where he's staying?"

Ziggy hesitated.

"Look. I was just kidding earlier. He has a tactical advantage. I need to know where he's staying to even the playing field. I'm not going to do anything stupid."

Ziggy said nothing while he studied me.

"Well?"

He removed his hat, ran a hand back through his hair, and sighed. "Town and Country Motel on 67. Room 12." He paused. "You didn't hear it from me."

A gun and a badge might come in handy if this Finn thing went sideways, but I needed to stall a little longer. Before I sware an oath to uphold the law, I might have to break it.

CHAPTER SIX

As the evening wore on and Alex kept nodding off in his chair, Hattie offered to take him home and put him to bed. She planned to stop by her house and pick up an overnight bag in case it turned out to be a long night at the hospital for me. Raven, who had been keeping Alex occupied, had gone home a couple of hours ago.

With too much time on my hands, I thought a lot about Ziggy's offer. I leaned a little more toward accepting and working part time if this Finn thing went on much longer. I can take care of myself if things get physical, but having access to the resources of the Teller County Sheriff's Department certainly wouldn't hurt.

Jenn was the wild card at this point. I had no way of knowing how much care she would need when she woke up. Zig was a good friend, and I didn't want to let him down, but Jenn would always come first.

I would attend Monday night's meeting as a favor to Zig. Jenn and I also had a vested interest in what was happening in Redfield. A big casino with an airport in our backyard was a very unwelcome prospect.

I Googled Riverdale on my phone and found they owned eleven properties in Montana, Wyoming, and Utah. Seven of their properties had opened within the last eighteen months.

They would identify a rural location with nearby infrastructure and buy up all the land by any means possible. They had a boatload of cash and often paid landowners twice the property's market value. Some saw it as progress—money, jobs, modern infrastructure—while others only saw the influx of outsiders, bringing crime and corruption that would destroy their peaceful way of life.

More often than not, a civil war would break out between those who wanted to sell and those who wanted to preserve that peaceful way. Riverdale's record with law enforcement during their expansion had been less than stellar.

The doctor appeared a little after midnight, looking haggard from the long day. I thanked him for hanging in there with us. He said Jenn was conscious but confused and warned me that her memory was sketchy. I followed him to her room.

I nearly burst into tears when I saw her. Not because of the tubes and wires, but because I hadn't been sure I'd ever be able to look into those beautiful eyes again.

"Hey," I said. "You gave us quite a scare. How are you feeling?"

"I've been better." Her speech was slower than normal. "Who's us?"

"Me and Alex for sure. Hattie, Raven, and Ziggy were here too."

She wore a puzzled look. "And you are...?"

I glanced at the doctor as Jenn waited for my answer. "I'm Dillon. We live together on the ranch with Alex, the eleven-year-old boy you adopted last year."

She studied me for a moment, then said, "Oh."

Was that, *oh, now I remember,* or *oh, that's news to me?* I couldn't tell.

The doctor nodded. "You can sit with her for a while if you like."

I pulled a chair next to the bed. Her blue eyes were vacant, with none of the usual sparkle. Fear crept in. Fear that they would never be as vibrant. I couldn't let my mind go there.

"Alex wanted to be here when you woke, but it's after midnight and he didn't make it. Hattie took him home and put him to bed."

Another "Oh."

"Are you in any pain?"

She eased her head from side to side. "My head hurts a little."

I should have asked how much medication she was on. I hoped it was the medication that made her act like... not Jenn.

"The doctor said you're going to be admitted and have to stay for a few days. I told him to put you in a private room."

She closed her eyes, and I slipped her hand into mine as it lay limp on the bed. We sat quietly. The touch of her skin calmed me, and I drifted off to sleep.

***

A nurse woke us up for the fourth time. I looked at my phone—seven-thirty. She checked Jenn's vitals and said the doctor had ordered another MRI and would be in with the results later.

"Is she doing any better?"

The nurse swiped at the iPad she'd brought in. "Her vitals are trending in the right direction. The doctor can tell you more after the MRI."

"When is the MRI?"

"They'll take her down after breakfast."

I looked at Jenn. Our eyes met, and I saw the flicker of an uncertain smile. Had she recognized me, or was she just being polite?

"How are you feeling?" I asked after the nurse left the room.

She eased her head from side to side and stretched her arms. "A little better, I guess."

"That's good." I hesitated. "Do you remember me?"

She nodded.

I smiled. Progress.

"You said your name was Dillon, right?"

My heart dropped into my stomach. I forced a smile. "That's right."

She didn't remember why she was in the hospital or how she got there. I told her about the helicopter, and she said she wished she remembered that. So did I.

Her breakfast arrived, and we continued our conversation between bites.

"Do you know a man named Finn Rafferty?"

She frowned as she stared at the wall across from her bed.

"You were married to him. Do you remember that?"

She nodded. "That's over now." She paused. "Isn't it?"

I wish I could tell her for sure. "I think so."

"I haven't seen him in years."

Long-term memory seemed better than short. "You worked in a thrift shop in Dallas."

"Yes, I remember. I loved that job. The shop was near the VA hospital. A lot of vets would stop in."

"Yes, very good. You sold a couple pairs of jeans and a Stetson to one of those vets, and he took you out for coffee after."

She turned to me, eyes wide. "You're that guy. You wore that hat while you tried on your britches. I told you it looked good on you."

"I reckon I *am* that good-looking guy. Dillon Bishop."

"Like the chess piece."

I smiled. "Exactly."

She finished her meal. She was either very hungry, or she'd forgotten what good food tasted like.

After breakfast, another nurse, or maybe a technician, wheeled her down to the imaging department for her MRI.

I threw some water on my face in the bathroom before walking to the cafeteria. After I ate, I roamed the halls to kill some time. I felt like this was my fault. Jenn didn't want to go on the ride. She wasn't feeling well, but I guilted her into it for Alex's sake. In my defense, I wouldn't have suggested it had I known she was pregnant. And I wasn't the one who insisted she ride a horse that wasn't ready to venture outside the pen.

I returned to an empty room. She should have been back by now. What was taking so long? I tried to sit but kept popping up every couple of minutes. I wasn't sure if it was nerves or the two cups of coffee I'd had with breakfast.

Mort called as I paced around her room. He asked to speak to Jenn. I told him what had happened and that she was having trouble with her memory.

"Do you know the name of her attorney?"

"I sure don't. I didn't even know she was married."

"I'm afraid she might still be."

I didn't like where this was going. "According to Jenn, that's impossible."

"That's why I need to speak to her attorney."

"Why? What's he going to tell you? You've seen the annulment papers. There legit, aren't they?"

"Yes but it's an interlocutory decree. That means it's provisional. It doesn't take effect until it is filed with the clerk. Her attorney should have done that, but I can't find any record of it."

"I'll ask her, but I wouldn't hold my breath. The doc said her memory was sketchy. That was an understatement. She didn't remember me at first." I had trouble talking about it. "After some prodding, she remembered meeting me in Dallas. There's that, but I'm not sure if we went home right now and walked into the bedroom together, she wouldn't throw me out of the house."

"Hmm... Well, I'll make some more inquiries. The court was in Leavenworth County, I'll start there."

I had hoped the conversation would go differently. Jenn couldn't be married. She just couldn't. I planned to ask her about the lawyer but keep the rest to myself.

Her smile was tentative when they wheeled her back in, but she still remembered me. I asked if she knew the name of the lawyer who worked on her annulment. As expected, she didn't have a clue.

Dr. Zacharia introduced himself and explained that Dr. Howard, who'd examined her last night, was off until later that evening. He assured us that he'd been brought up to speed on her case. The MRI results looked good, and he expected a full recovery. The dexamethasone that Dr. Howard had prescribed appeared to be shrinking the swollen brain tissue, decreasing the pressure that had been causing the bulk of her impairments. He said the full effects of the drug could take twenty-four to thirty-six hours.

I let out the breath I'd been holding since he began talking. His prognosis left the door open enough for hope to creep in.

Chapter Seven

I felt comfortable taking a break from my hospital vigil to attend the Riverdale meeting in the basement of the town hall. Hattie, God bless her, had watched Alex after Raven dropped him off from school. She planned to take him to see Jenn after dinner, then watch him at the house until I got home.

Ziggy nodded and smiled when I walked into the meeting room. He met me in the back and filled me in on the agenda. A crowd of interested people milled about the room, stopping to greet friends and express their opinions. I knew some faces, but not the names. A table with four empty chairs faced the audience at the front of the room.

Three men and one woman entered the room silently and took their seats in the front like contestants on a game show. I stood in the back so I could see the entire room. As I waited for the first contestant to speak, Finn walked in and took a seat up front.

Ziggy and Bill were in uniform and stationed on either side of the room. The presentation lasted about forty-five minutes, with a video and slick handouts. Each contestant had something to say about how the new casino and resort would benefit everyone there.

I wasn't sure how Finn fit into all this. He wasn't from around here and didn't own any land... unless he was still married to Jenn. His presence at the meeting told me he was at least interested, if not involved.

Jenn said Finn was a no-account con man who could sell ice to Eskimos. Maybe he was working for Riverdale. I had to wonder if they interviewed for sleazeballs, or if Finn slithered out from under a rock at one of their construction sites and they hired him on the spot. Jenn said he liked to gamble, so maybe he was working off a debt. Either way, this added an extra dimension to our Finn Rafferty dilemma back at the ranch.

By the time the presentation ended, the natives were getting restless. All hell broke loose during the Q & A session that followed. I noticed Finn stayed interested, but out of the fray. After each answer, people shouted out whatever was on their mind. The room was pretty evenly divided between the Hatfields and the McCoys.

I hated to bail on Ziggy in the middle of the chaos, but I didn't have a gun or badge, and there was someplace else I needed to go before this meeting broke up.

***

I drove south on Route 67 toward the Town and Country Motel. I'd been by the place a couple of times but never had occasion to stop in. Until now. I parked in the far corner of the lot where I still had a clear sight line to room 12. Unless they shut the meeting down early, I probably had a half hour.

Lights burned in several of the windows, but the parking lot was quiet and room 12 was dark. I picked the lock—extracurricular military training—and stepped inside. I pushed the curtain back a couple of inches and looked out. Still quiet.

The room looked bigger than I'd expected, with a kitchenette and a bistro table with two chairs. A small desk held a mess of papers, with more on the unmade bed.

I searched through the papers, mostly Riverdale memos and other correspondence printed from his laptop. There certainly appeared to be a Riverdale connection, which wasn't obvious from the meeting. Was he on their payroll? In what capacity? I unfolded a map and took pictures with my phone.

I rifled through the desk drawers, and things got personal. In an unmarked folder, I found surveillance photos of Jenn, Alex, and myself. I sat down on the desk chair and examined them. Most of the shots were taken in town. When I saw the ones taken at the ranch, it felt like somebody cinched my saddle too tight. The barn and stables, the cabins, multiple angles of the house, a couple of Buck, and a couple more of Alex playing with Romeo.

I couldn't understand how he could have done this without our knowledge. I needed to hire security, or at least get a dog.

I spread the photos out a few at a time and took more pictures. I didn't want Finn to know that I'd seen them, so I returned them to the folder and slipped them back in the drawer exactly where I found them.

I sat at the desk and opened the laptop. The sounds from the computer must have concealed the key being inserted in the door. Before I could react, Finn stood in the open doorway. We stared at each other for a moment. He must have been more surprised than me at this impromptu get together, but he recovered quickly.

"Find what you're looking for?"

"I just got here, so no." I paused. "What's the password?"

He didn't look amused.

"I saw you at the meeting," he said after an awkward pause. "Now I know why you left early."

"What are you doing in Redfield?" I asked.

"I have business here. Last I checked, it was a free country."

"What kind of business?"

"I'm not at liberty to discuss."

"You work for those casino people?"

"You ask a lot of questions for someone breaking the law."

I wanted to confront him about the photos, but I thought better of it.

"I'm disappointed." He shook his head slowly. "I thought perhaps we could become friends."

"What made you think we could ever be friends when you're trying to come between Jenn and me?"

"I'm afraid it's you who is trying to come between me and my wife."

"Jenn claims you're not married."

"She's mistaken." He paused. "Perhaps you could check with her attorney, a Mr. Cyrus T. Barnes." He frowned and tilted his head. "Oh, wait. He's dead."

I made a mental note of the name.

"I think you and I are very much alike," he continued. "A dreadful childhood full of disappointment and loss. Now that we've come out the other side, we vow to never let it happen again."

Lucky guess. "Not even close."

"I know more about you than you think, Mr. Bishop from Bradley, Texas."

Okay. I had been feeling sorry for the poor bastard, but now he was creeping me out.

"It's late, and I'm tired, so let's cut to the chase. Legally, I own half of the Red Valley Ranch. So, I have to ask myself, why am I living in this flea bag when I own a beautiful ranch a few miles up the road? It doesn't make sense."

I didn't like where this was going.

"So, I've been thinking," he continued. "There's plenty of room over there, what with those nice cabins down by the river, so tomorrow I plan to move my things into one of them."

My back stiffened. "Over my dead body."

"I hoped it wouldn't come to that."

He reached both hands behind his back and produced a Glock 9mm in one and a silencer in the other. I watched him screw the silencer on and set the piece on the table in front of him. If he was trying to scare me... it worked. I silently berated myself for not taking the pictures and getting the hell out of there when I had the chance.

"What are you going to do, shoot me?"

He paused a moment. If he'd had a mustache, he'd have been twirling the ends with his greasy fingers. "Let's see. A torrid affair turns deadly when husband is ambushed in hotel room. Story at eleven." A crooked grin snaked across his lips.

I tried, but I had no snappy comeback.

"Torrid affair. Hmm... Is that too much? If I recall, my little Jenny was a real tiger in the sack."

He didn't know it yet, but he had just made a Texas-size mistake. I feigned being crushed by his remark and hung my shoulders. He relaxed, and I sprung at him like a coiled-up rattlesnake.

I grabbed the edge of the table and pushed it up into his face. The gun flew into the air as he stumbled backward. I grabbed it in one hand and pushed the upended table aside with the other. He looked up at me with wide eyes as I stood over him, gun pointed at his chest.

"Easy, Sparky," I said. "Looks like you're going to have to stop the presses and rewrite that headline."

I couldn't trust that he didn't have another gun strapped to his ankle. I aimed the gun at his head while I patted down his legs.

"You look like a reasonable man..." he said, his voice shaky. "Present situation excluded, of course. Maybe we can help each other."

"I doubt it, unless you're talking about me helping you out of town."

"Jenny kicked me to the curb years ago, and I probably deserved it. She's better off without me. I've simply come to claim the marital property that is rightfully mine."

"You want half the ranch."

"If Jenny could somehow be persuaded to let me sell my half, we could all walk away from this mess."

"That's not going to happen."

"When I get the deed to my half of the land, I'll sign divorce papers, and she'll be all yours."

"You need to listen to me carefully." I tightened my grip on the gun. "I don't care what you think in that twisted little mind of yours, but you and Jenn are done. You don't own shit."

"You don't understand. They're going to kill me if—"

"Stay away from her... and the ranch."

I released the clip into my hand and shoved it into my back pocket. "I'll be back tomorrow, and I better not find you here."

I tossed the gun onto the bed and walked out the door.

Chapter Eight

I returned home to find Hattie with Alex, in his PJs, watching television. Alex bolted off the couch when he saw me and told me about his hospital visit. Hattie smiled as she watched us from her seat.

We made a deal that he could finish the show if he let me talk with Hattie in the kitchen.

"I think she's doing much better," Hattie said. "The doctor agreed."

"Did she recognize Alex?"

"I wasn't sure at first, but she called him by name several times. I'd never mentioned his name."

I nodded approval. "Maybe I should go see her."

"No offense, but I think she's had enough excitement for one day. They gave her something to help her sleep when we left." Her expression turned serious. "I think Alex needs to get back to his old routine. You should put him to bed and be here in the morning when he wakes up."

I tried unsuccessfully to suppress a yawn.

"You need a good night's sleep yourself."

"I guess you're right."

I thanked her and gave her a big hug. She said goodnight to Alex, and I walked her to her car. A light burned in Buck's window, and I wanted to bring him up to speed on everything that had happened that day, but I didn't want to leave the house unguarded.

Finn struck me as all hat and no cattle, but I'd pushed him hard tonight. I didn't want to let my guard down. A cornered rat will bite the cat. Even if this rat left town, I had a feeling he wouldn't go far. This wasn't over.

Alex and I talked for a while about Jenn before I read him a story and kissed him goodnight. Downstairs, I removed Pop's .45 caliber pistol from the gun cabinet. I loaded a clip, chambered a round, and checked the safety.

***

Morning arrived quickly and without incident. Alex fixed his own breakfast, and I waited with him at the end of the driveway for the school bus. I found Buck in the barn after Alex had been picked up.

"We need to talk," I said.

"How's Jenny doing?"

"A little better. I'll find out more when I see her this morning."

Buck shook his head. "Terrible thing that happened to her."

"I found where Finn's been staying."

He raised an eyebrow. "Where?"

"Doesn't matter. He's leaving. I broke in last night and was going through his stuff when he surprised me."

"What'd ya do?"

"He pulled a gun, but I was able to turn the tables. I told him to leave town. I think he got the message this time."

I told Buck about the correspondence I'd found between Finn and Riverdale.

"He won't go far if he's workin' for them casino people."

"Yeah, maybe I should have let him stay where I can keep an eye on him. But he said some things about Jenn that got my tail up, and before you know it, I had a gun to his head, tossin' around ultimatums. I'm gonna swing by there later and see if he cleared out."

"Did you find anything else?"

I pulled out my phone, located the pictures I'd taken, and handed it to him. "Found these in his room."

Buck's mustache twitched as he flipped through the pictures. "That son of a bitch." He stopped to blow out a breath. "He's makin' us look like fools. When do you reckon he took these?"

"Don't know."

He handed the phone back. "When you're through, I'd like a piece of him."

"If there's anything left." I slipped the phone into my pocket. "We need better security around here."

"What are you proposin'?

"We could hire somebody, or get a watchdog, or..."

"Or what?"

"What if we parked a patrol car in front of the house every night?"

"How you gonna manage that?"

I held up a *wait-a-minute-and-I'll-show-you* finger and pulled out my phone. Ziggy answered on the second ring.

"When do I start?"

***

Amid all this chaos, I found myself tapping the steering wheel and humming an old Garth Brooks tune as I pulled into the hospital parking lot. I needed to keep my thoughts positive. Jenn would be back to normal in no time. I couldn't wait to see her.

Jenn was sitting up in bed, and I could tell immediately that some of the sparkle had returned to her eyes. They lit up with recognition when I walked into her room.

"Hi, Dillon."

I know it sounds corny, but my heart skipped a beat or two. "Hey, Babe. If you ain't a site for sore eyes. You're feeling better, I reckon."

"Well, my head doesn't hurt like it did, and I have a hankerin' for a big ol' cheeseburger and some of them twisty fries."

I must have looked like a prize turkey on the day after Thanksgiving. "When does the doc say you can come home?"

"Why don't you ask him yourself?"

I turned around to see Doc Zacharia standing in the doorway behind me.

"Hey, Doc. How's she doing?"

"I'm happy to report she is recovering nicely. The medication and osmotherapy have reduced her swelling, and her memory and cognitive functions are improving."

"That's great news." I glanced at Jenn, then back at the doctor. "When can I take her home?"

He frowned. "I'd like to monitor her one more night. If she continues to improve, I'll discharge her tomorrow."

I nodded.

"She'll need to take things easy for the next week or two. She may have intermittent episodes of confusion, fatigue, and irritability, so be patient with her."

"You bet."

He examined Jenn, asked her a few questions, then continued with his rounds.

"Did you hear that?" I asked Jenn after he'd left the room.

She nodded. "How's Alex doing?"

"Good. He misses you and keeps asking when you're coming home."

"The doctor said tomorrow, right?"

"That's what he said." I wanted to ask her if the name Cyrus Barnes meant anything to her, but I figured that could wait another day. I didn't want to press my luck.

I stayed with her until her lunch arrived. I promised to buy her a cheeseburger and some twisty fries tomorrow.

Chapter Nine

I drove to the sheriff's office in Divide. Ziggy met me at the door, excited to welcome me aboard. After I took the oath to support 'the Laws and Constitution of the United States of America and the State of Colorado', he issued me my badge, sidearm, uniform, and the keys to my patrol vehicle.

He said I could work part time, every other day, starting tomorrow. I held him off for a day so I could spend some time helping Jenn transition back to life at home.

I tried on my uniform when I got home, including the government-issued Stetson. As I looked at myself in the mirror, my eyes were drawn to the shiny star pinned to my chest. Bittersweet memories of my little brother, Luke, played in my mind like clips from an old movie.

I was nine, and Luke was seven. For Halloween that year, he wanted to be Sheriff of Johnson County, and Mama obliged. He had trouble with the star, so I helped pin it on his chest. He wore that uniform proudly—for over a week. We called him *Lawman Luke*, and he couldn't get enough. Pop finally put his foot down a week later.

Luke disappeared when we were in high school, and the case went cold. I served two tours in Afghanistan, then nearly lost my life when I returned stateside and pushed a little too hard to reopen his case. Eventually, all our questions were answered, and we finally put him to rest.

I found that costume years later in a box at the bottom of Pop's closet. I kept that little tin star so the spirit of Lawman Luke might guide me through some difficult times. He never let me down, and that star remains the only memento I have from my childhood.

Today, I got to wear the real thing. I'd be lying if I said I couldn't wait for Jenn to see me in uniform. I decided I would wear it to the hospital when I picked her up in the morning. Maybe I would carry her out of there like Richard Gere in the final scene of *An Officer and a Gentleman*.

I'd left my truck at the station so I could try out my new ride—a late-model Ford Bronco. I reckoned I should test the lights and siren on the way home. I tracked down Buck to ask if I could hitch a ride back to pick it up.

"Can I help you, Officer?" Buck said when I walked into the barn.

I smiled and held my arms out at my sides. "What do you think?"

"I think I'm gonna run over to my place and hide all the contraband."

"I'll look the other way if you do me a favor. I need you to drive me up to Divide so I can pick up my truck."

"Now?"

"Raven dropped Alex off at Hattie's after school, so I need to pick him up before dinner."

"That your patrol car I seen parked out front?"

"It sure is. I'm thinking it might keep some of the riffraff off the ranch."

Buck smiled. "Hope it don't scare away the ranch hands."

"If it does, we didn't need 'em anyway."

He took a quick look around the barn. "I reckon I can go with you, but we'll need to take your new ride. My truck had a flat yesterday, and the spare's balder than an eagle. She's one wrong turn away from the junkyard, besides."

At the station, I tossed him the keys to my truck and told him I'd meet him back at the ranch. I had an errand to run before I picked up Alex.

Gravel crunched under my tires as I turned into the Town and Country Motel parking lot. Finn's car was nowhere in sight. A good sign. I parked in front of room 12 and walked up to the door. Knocking several times produced no answer. Another good sign. I headed for the office.

"Afternoon, Officer," said a fifty-something man with round glasses and long hair. He could have been John Denver's brother. "What can I do you for?"

A picture on the wall told me he owned the place. He stood behind a counter that held one rack of touristy brochures and another of travel-size sundry items. Soda and snack vending machines anchored one paneled wall while the other was home to a couple of waiting-room-style chairs.

Funny how everyone is so polite when you're wearing a uniform. My first impression is always that they're hiding something. I probably needed to work on that.

I nodded and tipped my hat. "I'm looking for some information on the man in room 12. Let's start with if he's still here."

"We don't usually give out information like that."

Maybe I should stick with first impressions. "You really shouldn't, but it's part of an investigation, and I'm asking you nice. I can come back with a warrant."

"No need for that."

He shuffled some papers on the counter. A row of keys hung on the wall behind him. Several of the hooks were empty. Number twelve was not. A locked display case below them appeared to offer various edible marijuana items for sale. A closer look at his eyes gave me reason to believe he'd been eating into the profits on his way to a rocky mountain high.

"Here it is." He glanced up at me and smiled, like his cooperation might keep the building inspector away. "A Mr. Rafferty checked out this morning."

"When did he check in?"

He flipped a few pages. "He's been here going on four months."

"Let me guess. He paid cash."

"On time, every week." He smiled like that wasn't the norm.

"Did he say where he might be going?"

"Like I told that other fella, that's one of them *don't, ask don't tell* kinda things, which is okay by me."

"Someone else was in here asking about Rafferty?"

"Yesterday. Big ugly guy. I told him we don't give out that kind of information. He didn't take too kindly to that."

I pointed to the security camera in the corner of the room. "I'm going to need to see the video from that."

"Sure thing. Installed that myself." His grin gave me the impression of a proud papa. "It'll take me a couple of minutes to cue it up."

I nodded and followed him into a utility room behind the desk. He sat at a computer screen and tapped a few keys. The motel office appeared on the black-and-white screen and flickered as he rewound the video. Watching the timestamp in the corner, he slowed it down and eventually stopped it when a large man entered through the front door.

"That's him," he said, pointing at the screen.

I leaned over his shoulder to get a better look. "Can I get a screenshot of that?"

He tapped a key, then turned to me with a grin. "Should come off that little printer any minute now."

I studied the black-and-white picture that I retrieved from the tray. No one I recognized.

"Hope that helps, Officer."

"It does, thanks," I said and let myself out.

Finn was gone, but how far and for how long? I second-guessed running him out of town, especially if it saved him from a beating, or worse, from Big Ugly Guy.

My best friend, Coop, would be disappointed. He always said, "Keep your friends close, and your enemies closer." Okay, I'd scared him away, but there was another Riverdale meeting next week, and I fully expected to see Finn there.

I drove to Hattie's place to pick up Alex.

Hattie looked me up and down. "If I were twenty years younger…"

I smiled and held my arms out at my sides. "Right?"

"I hear Jenn's coming home tomorrow."

"That's the plan." I paused. "I really want to thank you for all you've done while she's been down."

She waved a dismissing hand, jangling her bracelets. "It was nothin'. You three are like family. I'm just glad she's better."

"I reckon I owe you one, anyway."

"How's Buck?"

"Still Buck," I said with a shrug.

Her eyes drifted for a moment. "That's not such a bad thing."

I arched an eyebrow. "Something you're not telling me?"

"I made you two some shepherd's pie for dinner. It's still warm, but you might want to put it in the oven for a bit when you get home."

"You didn't have to."

"I know."

I thanked her a few more times before we left.

Alex's eyes lit up when he saw my new ride. "Wow! Are we going to ride home in that?"

I couldn't help but smile. "All the way."

***

I waited with Alex at the end of the driveway for the school bus the next morning. He awoke all excited about Jen's homecoming and begged me to let him come with me to pick her up. I almost caved, but someone had to be the parent in Jenn's absence.

Ziggy called on my walk back to the house.

"I need you to work today."

"I thought we agreed I could have the day off to be with Jenn."

"There's been an incident at the hospital. I need you to meet me here."

I stopped walking. "Is Jenn alright?"

"Just get here as soon as you can."

I don't remember ending the call. I hightailed it to the house and threw on my uniform. Gravel flew as I backed out and tore down the drive. I turned on the siren when I reached the road.

Ziggy met me at the front door. "Jenn's going to be fine."

I let out the breath that it felt like I'd been holding since his phone call. "I want to see her."

He held up his hands as I attempted to push past him. "You can't just yet."

"Why?"

"She's in the OR."

"Surgery? What for? She was supposed to go home today."

Ziggy took my arm. "Let's sit."

My pulse raced, and I tugged at my collar, which seemed to tighten by the minute. "What happened?"

"As far as we can tell, someone impersonating a nurse entered Jenn's room and injected her with what they believe was succinylcholine. Fortunately, a real nurse stopped her before she could get it all in. They fought briefly, before the perp fled."

"What does this succino—whatever it's called—do?"

"From what I could gather, it's a muscle relaxer. Too much can cause you to stop breathing."

"Is that what happened?"

"It appears that way, but they were able to revive her quickly."

Ziggy put his hand on my shoulder. "Dillon..."

My brain had trouble processing all this. I turned. He had a worried look in his eyes that made me wonder what he'd been holding back.

"The baby wasn't so lucky."

I bolted to my feet. "She lost it?"

Ziggy stood and put his hands on my shoulders. "I'm afraid so."

I shook loose and took a step back.

"I'm sorry, Dillon."

"Who would do this?" I didn't expect an answer. I had a pretty good idea. "What are we doing standing around here? We need to find whoever did this and—"

"I know this is difficult, Dillon, but you need to hold it together. You need to be strong for Jenn... and Alex."

I knew he was right. I had a tendency to let my fear and rage get the better of me. One night, when Jenn and I were staying at Pop's hunting cabin on Lake Whitney, I flashed back to Afghanistan. I lost all sense of time and place. Choppers and enemy gunfire sounded in the distance. After I shot up the woods with one of Pop's hunting rifles, I barricaded myself inside the house. In the morning, when I couldn't find Jenn, I panicked, fearing she might be dead at my hands. She'd spent the night hiding in my truck, unable—or maybe unwilling—to go back in the house.

This wasn't that, but I recognized it as a possible trigger. I took a couple of deep breaths. "She needs protection. You need to post someone outside her door."

"I'm sorry. I just don't have the manpower." He sighed. "You're all I've got, and there's no way I'm going to assign you that duty."

"Why not?"

"You're too emotionally involved." He placed a hand on my shoulder. "I'll stay here today if you'll go back to the station and hold down the fort."

"I appreciate that, but I need to be out there looking for whoever did this."

He tightened his grip on my shoulder. "No. I need you back at the station. I'll look at the security tapes while I'm here." He met my gaze. "Jenn will most likely be sedated for a while. I'll keep you posted."

I said nothing as a few seconds passed. He hadn't yet figured out that, since my discharge from the army, I wasn't very good at taking orders.

Chapter Ten

I stopped at the end of the hospital driveway. A left turn would bring me to the sheriff's station. I turned right. If the county couldn't provide adequate security for Jenn, I would have to find someone who could.

Jacob and Jeremiah Whitehawk had become well-known troublemakers in these parts after their mother, Asha Whitehawk, died in a car driven by Jenn's Uncle Roy. They didn't hide their contempt for the man they believed killed their mother. When Roy's barn burned down, they went to prison for it, even though they didn't do it. They continued to blame him until I proved otherwise. I even let them get a few good licks in on the actual killer before Ziggy hauled him off to jail.

I planned to make the Whitehawks an offer to move into one of the cabins and provide round-the-clock security until we figured out who wanted to kill Jenn and why. Buck's relationship with the boys had always been less than cordial, and I figured they would be as welcome as a porcupine at a nudist colony. I'd grown to like that crusty old cowboy, but right now he wasn't my first priority.

Asha's sister, Cassidy, owned a café on the main drag of a small village that a tribe of Cheyenne established on land given to them by Uncle Roy after Asha's death. She was my only link to the brothers, who kept a low profile.

The little bell that jingled when I walked in reminded me of Hattie's. The place was nearly full with the lunch rush. I felt their stares as I read the large menu on the wall behind the counter, which indicated that they served a variety of caffeinated beverages along with light breakfast and lunch fare.

Cassidy's big ebony eyes stared as I approached the counter. "Dillon?"

I nodded, aware that she'd never seen me in uniform. I removed my hat and held it in front of me with both hands.

"You the law now?"

"Imagine that." I smiled. "I'm looking for your nephews."

Her expression fell. "What did they do this time?"

"Oh, no... it's not like that. I want to hire them to provide security at the ranch."

Amusement quickly replaced her relief. "Really?"

"I thought I could make honest men out of them... at least for a couple of weeks."

"They could sure use the help."

She offered me a cup of coffee, which I politely declined.

"I need to get back."

"I'll get you one to go, then."

"Sure." I watched her pour a cup and snap on a plastic lid. "Will you help me?"

"When can they start?"

I set my hat on top of my head and gave it a tap, then picked up the cup from the counter. "Have them meet me at the ranch in an hour."

She nodded. "They'll be there."

On the way back to the ranch, I radioed the dispatcher and told her I'd be in as soon as I'd arranged security for this morning's hospital victim.

"Have you heard from Ziggy?" I asked.

"Just to say he'd be at the hospital until further notice."

"Roger that. I'll see you in a couple of hours."

I pulled up to the barn and called Buck's name when I got out. He hollered something from inside. I waited until he appeared out of the dark mouth of the barn into the sunlight.

"All quiet around here?" I asked.

"About as exciting as a mashed-potato sandwich."

I frowned. I had to think about that one for a moment. "That's good. We don't want any more excitement."

He produced a dirty rag and wiped his nose a couple of times.

"I'm thinking of hiring the Whitehawk brothers for on-site security when I bring Jenn home."

"On site?"

"They're gonna stay in one of the cabins."

Buck's bushy gray eyebrows nearly touched as he frowned.

"Look, I know you guys have had your differences in the past, but I thought things were better since we resolved the Roy thing."

"They tracked me down like a dog when I left last year."

"I hired them to find you. Those two could track a rattlesnake through the Grand Canyon. It's in their blood. They were just doing their job." I let the words hang there. "You packed up your shit and snuck out of town in the middle of the night. You had information that I needed."

"Well... We ain't still trying to kill each other. That's all I'll say." His mustache twitched. "Why all the security?"

I met his gaze. "Someone tried to kill Jenn this morning."

"What? In the hospital?" He shifted his weight, like if he didn't, he might tumble over. "Judas Priest! Who would do such a thing?"

"I'm working on that."

"How can I help?"

"Make sure one of the cabins is cleaned up and ready for them to move in."

He shook his head. "I'm not sure I like the idea of them hooligans livin' here."

"It's just for a couple of weeks. I need them here to keep an eye on things."

"Who's gonna keep an eye on *them*?"

"I know it won't be easy for you." I put a hand on his shoulder and squeezed. "Do it for Jenn."

Buck pressed his lips together and nodded. If I didn't know him better, I'd say he was fixin' to burst into tears.

He wiped his nose again and disappeared into the mouth of the barn. My phone rang.

"Hey, Mort."

"Dillon, I've got some bad news."

***

I stood in front of the barn with my phone up to my ear, listening to silence, not sure how long ago the call had ended. I reckoned about the same time my life ended, and my world came crashing down around me.

According to Mort, I was sleeping with a married woman. My words, not his. He'd done some research and found no record of the annulment filing anywhere in the state of Kansas. He had a copy of the decree from a judge in Leavenworth, but apparently that didn't mean squat unless it was filed.

Jenn's attorney, Cyrus Barnes, who was supposed to file it, was dead, just as Finn had said. I didn't like the snarky way he'd said it, almost like he knew we would be looking for the man. Like he knew why the papers hadn't been filed. Something didn't smell right. Mort promised to dig a little deeper into why Jenn's annulment never got filed. I ended the call without telling him about the attempt on her life.

Poor Jenn. I didn't know what was worse, recovering from the attack, or finding out she was still married to that weasel Finn Rafferty. I was the one who would have to tell her. That was a conversation I was not looking forward to.

When I called the hospital to check on Jenn, they told me she was resting in her room. She wasn't safe at the hospital. Ziggy didn't have enough manpower to post a guard at her door 24/7, so I planned to get her out of there. I inquired about hiring a nurse to tend to Jenn for a few days here at the ranch.

Jacob and Jeremiah arrived twenty minutes later, and we talked about my expectations and their compensation. They weren't as bad as people made them out to be. They'd been dealt a crappy hand with the loss of their mother. Anytime something bad happened around town they were at the top of the suspect list. They spent a lot of time down at the Wet Whistle, so there's that.

After we negotiated a deal, I took them down to one of the cabins and had Buck get them settled in. The three of them had never gotten along, and Buck gave me the stink eye when I left him alone with them to go to the hospital.

On my way to the hospital, I made arrangements for Alex to be dropped off at Hattie's after school. When I arrived, I found Jenn speaking with a nurse in her room. She looked better than I expected, all things considered.

"Where's Ziggy?" I asked.

"He said he was going downstairs to look at the security video from this morning."

Jenn introduced me to Maria Sanchez, the nurse who saved her life. I thanked her a couple dozen times and told her that her family was welcome anytime at the ranch to ride the horses.

Jenn looked at me. "They told Maria that you inquired about hiring a nurse to take care of me for a few days. Is that true?"

I nodded. "You can't stay here, and I thought it would be better if you had someone who knows more than me around until you get back on your feet."

"Why can't I stay here?"

"You're not safe here. Whoever did this might try again. I'm going to take you home today."

"Can you do that?"

"I already spoke with the doctor. They call it AMA, against medical advice. It's a thing."

Maria interjected. "I can help you."

"Thank you, but what about your job?"

"My supervisor wants me to take some time off, but I can't afford it."

"Tell you what," I said. "You take a week off, and I'll pay you double what they're paying you here."

Maria's eyes widened, and Jenn nodded her approval.

"We have a deal, then?"

She nodded enthusiastically. "Thank you, Mr. Bishop."

"You can call me Dillon." I raised an eyebrow. "I'm going to need you to start tomorrow."

I turned to Jenn after Maria left. She seemed pleased with the arrangement.

CHAPTER ELEVEN

Jenn pitched a fit when a nurse tried to wheel her out to the car, so I knew she was feeling better. I called Hattie to tell her we were on our way to pick up Alex. She told me they were back at the ranch fixin' us dinner. That woman is a real peach.

Alex wouldn't let go of Jenn when we walked in the house. He didn't know about the attempt on her life, he was just happy to have her back home. Hattie gave her a big hug and told her she'd made her famous meatloaf for our dinner tonight.

"Thanks, Hattie." I hooked a thumb toward Alex, who was still hanging from Jenn's neck. "I hope he wasn't any trouble."

"No trouble at all." She paused. "I saw a couple of Indians roaming around the ranch when I got here."

"Jacob and Jeremiah."

"I didn't recognize them under all that war paint."

"What?"

"Relax." Her lips curled into a playful smile. "Buck told me you hired them to keep an eye on things around here. I think it's a good idea."

"I also have a nurse starting tomorrow. She'll stay with Jenn during the day until she's feeling better."

"You make it sound like I need a sitter," Jenn said.

Hattie looked at Jenn. "Hush, dear. Your man is just taking good care of you."

I turned to Alex. "Go wash your hands for dinner."

When he left the room, I continued. "I hired Maria Sanchez. The nurse who saved Jenn's life."

"In that case," Hattie said. "Maybe I'll come over another night and make dinner for all of you."

Hattie should run a restaurant instead of a hardware store. I asked her to stay and eat with us, but she politely declined. I watched Alex during dinner. He smiled so hard, it's a wonder any of the food stayed in his mouth.

My smile faded as I thought about the conversation Jenn and I would inevitably have. I wanted to give her more time to recover before I dropped the bomb that would blow her world apart, but I'd never hear the end of it if I held on to that kind of information.

I thought about waiting until the following day when we had a nurse on site, but after we put Alex to bed, I broached the subject.

"Mort called today," I said after Jenn sat on the edge of the bed.

As soon as I said it, she burst into tears.

Did she already know? "Are you okay?"

"Dillon, we lost our baby."

I sat next to her and put my arm around her trembling shoulders. I hadn't seen her break down yet, and I'd wondered when it would finally hit her. I knew nothing I could say would make it any easier, I just had to be there with her.

"I'm sorry. Let it out, Babe. I'm not going anywhere."

"It's not fair." The tears flowed freely, and I got her a box of tissues. "It was too soon to tell if it was a boy or a girl. We'll never know who that little person was."

We sat there until she spent every last ounce of energy and fell asleep on my shoulder. The nurse had given me some mild sedatives in case Jenn had trouble falling asleep. She didn't need any tonight. Eventually, I took off her shoes and got her settled under the covers. My bad news would have to wait until morning.

Someone would pay for this, one way or another. I needed some air... and a drink, so I threw on a jacket, grabbed Mr. Beam, and sat on the front porch swing. I couldn't remember the last time I cried. My tears had all been used up by the time I reached high school. Losing family had become a way of life. I didn't like it, but that's just the way it was. Maybe I'd grieve someday, but I had a score to settle first.

Jeremiah Whitehawk appeared out of the shadows, like a ghost in the night. I hadn't checked on the boys, so I was glad to see they weren't holding down their usual stools at the Wet Whistle. I gave him a nod, and he moved on without a sound.

My thoughts circled back to Jenn. I screwed the cap on the bottle and headed for bed. I didn't want to take the chance she might wake up alone.

****

Jenn woke early and took a shower. I feared she would spend the day in bed with the covers pulled over her head, so I considered this a good start. Maria arrived a little before eight o'clock, and I offered her a cup of coffee as I poured my second. I introduced her to Alex before walking him to the bus stop.

On my way back to the house, I called Ziggy.

"Jenn had a rough night last night, so I need to stay with her today."

His silence gave me the impression that my career as a deputy sheriff was off to a shaky start.

"Can you stop by the ranch? There's something I need to show you."

"You're in luck. I have some business in Redfield this morning. I can be at your place in half an hour."

Back inside, the three of us made small talk in the kitchen over another cup of coffee. I needed to tell Jenn the bad news, but I didn't know how to begin that conversation. Fortunately, I didn't have to.

"Last night you told me someone named Mort called." Jenn frowned. "Who is he again?"

Her memory wasn't getting any better. I hoped she couldn't see the disappointment in my eyes. "Mort is Mama's friend. He's the lawyer who's looking into the annulment thing."

"Oh. What did he say?"

I had to tell her. "It's not good news."

She closed her eyes and took in a deep breath, then blew it out slowly. She opened her eyes, and they told me to continue.

"I'm not sure how to say this..."

"Just give it to me straight."

Maria got up and rinsed her empty cup.

"The annulment was never filed. You're still married."

The color drained from her face, and I thought her breakfast was about to make another appearance. "That can't be right. Are you sure?"

"Mort did the research. There's no record of the decree ever being filed. It has to be filed to be legal."

"This can't be happening. I want to go back to sleep and start this day over. Hell, might as well make it the week."

I wished it was that easy.

Jenn jumped up from the table and threw up in the sink. Maria was at her side before I knew what was happening.

"Maybe she should get some rest," Maria said, suggesting that our conversation was over.

Jenn wiped her mouth with the back of her hand. She turned to me. "What am I going to do?"

"*We* are going to figure this out."

Jenn said she needed to lie down, so Maria took her upstairs. I waited for Ziggy in the living room.

"Thanks for coming," I said when he stepped in off the porch.

He removed his hat. "How's Jenn?"

"Not great. Her memory is still sketchy. She's upstairs resting."

"Well, you give her my best."

He followed me into the kitchen. "So, what did you want to show me?"

He declined my offer for coffee, and we sat at the table. I opened the picture app on my phone and handed it to him. "Go ahead, there's a bunch of 'em."

Ziggy flipped through the photos, stopping now and then. "How did you get these?"

"I met Finn the other night at his motel room."

"You expect me to believe that he just handed these over to you?" He frowned as he flipped through them again.

"I might have gotten there a little before he did."

"You mean you broke into his room."

"Technically, I didn't break anything."

"You can't be doing this kind of shit anymore, you understand?"

"Yes, sir."

"You're an officer of the law now. You're going to have to do things by the book."

"You mean like a warrant, or probable cause?"

"At least you've been *reading* the book."

"We need to arrest him," I said.

"Taking pictures isn't a crime, at least not around here."

"What about trespassing?"

"There's no way to prove who took these pictures."

Jenn appeared in the doorway. "What pictures?"

I cringed. I hadn't shown her the pictures. She was teetering on the edge of an emotional cliff, and I didn't want to push her over the edge.

I stood. "It's nothing, Babe. Just sheriff's department stuff." I shifted my weight. "Maybe you should go back to bed."

She set her jaw. "Don't handle me, Dillon. Just tell me what you're looking at."

"Okay. Maybe you'd better sit down."

Ziggy handed me the phone, and I gave it to Jenn.

The little color she had, drained from her face as she swiped the screen. Her breath became deeper, and her finger moved faster before dropping the phone on the table. "Who took these?"

I gave Ziggy a sideways glance. "I think it was Finn."

"We don't know that for sure." His remark came with a stern look.

"Whoever took these was here on the ranch."

"I know. That's why I hired security. The Whitehawk brothers are staying in one of the cabins until we get this sorted out."

Another stern look from Ziggy.

Jenn looked at Ziggy, then me. "What does he want?"

I met her gaze. "The ranch."

Chapter Twelve

Ziggy held up his hands. "We're not sure what he wants, But I'll make it a priority to find out."

I raised an eyebrow. "Don't you mean *we*?"

"We need to tread lightly, Dillon, and I'm not sure that's something you can do right now. You're too emotionally involved for me to trust your decision-making process."

"Who is more motivated to solve this case than me?"

"I'm not questioning your motivation."

I reckoned that was a diplomatic way of saying he didn't want to have a loose cannon on his hands. "Did you find anything on the hospital security videos?"

He removed a 5x7 print from the notebook he came in with. "We've got one clear shot of her entering the building." He slid it across the table. "You recognize her?"

I studied it, taking a mental picture of her face. I shook my head, then handed the photo to Jenn.

I hadn't shared the picture taken by the motel camera with Ziggy. To be honest, I hoped Big Ugly Guy would find Finn before we did and save us all a lot of trouble.

"I think she was one of my nurses," Jenn said. "Why would she want to kill me?"

"Someone else wanted you dead and hired her to do it."

"Why would anyone…" Her voice trailed off into a long silence.

Ziggy turned to me. "Have any theories?"

"I'm working on one." I paused for a moment, deciding on how much to tell them. "I think Finn is behind this."

Jenn glared at me like she knew I would accuse him.

"Go on," Ziggy said.

"Wait." Jenn straightened in her chair. "Finn's a con man and a royal douchebag, but I don't think he would kill me."

"Exactly. He's a con man. What motivates a con man? Money. You're sitting on a gold mine here. He wants a piece of it."

"Why now? Where's he been for the past eight years?"

"I don't have it all worked out yet, but you've only had the ranch for a year. Could Seth have told him?"

"They didn't know each other." She stood and walked to the sink, and I thought she might throw up again. Instead, she filled a glass with water, took a long drink, and turned around. "How did Finn know we were still married?" She paused. "I didn't know, and I wouldn't have told him, even if I'd known."

"I don't know." I glanced at Ziggy writing in his notebook.

"If he knew we were still married, I would have heard from him before now."

"Maybe you were of no use to him until you inherited the ranch."

Another glare.

"I meant no disrespect. The property transfer was public record." I looked at Ziggy, and he nodded.

"Finn's in some kind of trouble. He said *they* would kill him. That's why he needs the money he could get from selling his half of the ranch. But he didn't say who *they* were."

"If he thinks he's gettin' one dime out of me, he's dumber than a watermelon."

"I'm just telling you what he told me."

Jenn tilted her head. "When did he tell you all this?"

Oops! I realized that I'd never mentioned our little get-to-gether at Finn's motel. "Uh... I may have paid him a little visit the other night."

"And you're just telling me now?"

I held up my hands. "You were in the hospital. You had enough to deal with at the moment."

"He won't be doing that again," Ziggy said.

"I reckon I won't," I said. "I chased him out of town. Don't know where he went."

Ziggy leaned back in his chair, apparently lost for words. Jenn didn't have any, either. We sat in silence for a few minutes until a knock on the door startled us.

I went to the door and found Jacob and Jeremiah on the porch. Jacob held another man by the collar.

"We found him snooping around up north by the burial ground."

Uncle Roy, Asha Whitehawk, and Hattie's stillborn son were buried in a small, private cemetery at the north end of the property. The entire valley was visible from the cliffs up there.

The man stood about six feet tall, brown hair, average build. Blood had dried on his lip beneath some pretty deep scratches above one eye. I hadn't gotten a good look at the snowmobiler the other day, so I didn't know if it was the same man.

"That's private property," I said. "What were you doing up there?"

His eyes widened when he saw the sheriff walk into the room. Jenn followed.

"Was he on a snowmobile?"

Jacob nodded. "It's still up there."

Ziggy stepped forward. "Any chance you fellas can retrieve that sled for us?"

They both nodded.

"If it's registered, we might be able to find out who he is or who he's working for."

Jenn's eyes held a mix of fear and determination as she watched the scene unfold.

"In the meantime..." Ziggy pulled a pair of cuffs from his belt. "You're under arrest for trespassing."

"Thanks," I said to the boys before they left.

Ziggy turned to me. "I could use your help at the station."

"I'll take good care of her," Maria said.

I looked at Jenn. After a moment of hesitation, she nodded. "I'll be okay."

***

I changed into my uniform and waited for the boys to bring the sled down to the barn. Before I loaded it on a trailer and hauled it to the station, I called the information in to Ziggy. He had a name by the time I got there.

"James Dallarosa. No priors. He works for a small land management company in Montana."

"Why was he on our land?"

"He's not talking. My guess is it has something to do with the casino project."

"What are you going to do with him?"

"That depends. You think Jenn will press charges?"

"Probably."

"I can hold him for twenty-four hours while she decides. In the meantime, I'll try to contact his boss and find out what he's doing so far from home." He shuffled a few papers on his desk before looking up. "Want to take a ride?"

"Where to?"

"I got a call from the sheriff in Park County. I sent the picture we got from hospital security to the neighboring counties. He thinks he found our girl dead in a car in Fairplay."

"Murdered?"

"Looks that way. Bullet to the head."

I thought it ironic that someone would get killed in a town named Fairplay. "Let's go."

We ate lunch on the way, arriving in Fairplay an hour later. The Park County sheriff met us in the parking lot of a rundown, pay-by-the-hour motel off Highway 285. Ziggy introduced me and we ducked under the police tape that surrounded an area in the back. A dark gray sedan sat next to a dumpster. As we approached, I saw blood splattered on the inside of the driver's window. The passenger door hung open.

"Looks like the driver took one to the right side of the head from close range. Nine millimeter, if I had to guess. At first, I thought robbery." The sheriff glanced over at the building. "But given the location, that's unlikely."

"Looks like a pay 'n' play motel. Could be sex related." I said. "Maybe an unsatisfied customer?"

He shrugged. "I got the coroner and a tech from the crime lab on their way over here."

"Did you ask if anyone inside knew her or saw her last night?"

"Nobody recognized her, but until we establish time of death, we might be asking the wrong people."

"I did a quick check of the vehicle compartment," he continued. "No cell phone or purse."

"Can we have a look?" Ziggy asked.

"Like I said, CSU hasn't been here, so don't touch anything."

I followed Ziggy to the open passenger door. He pulled Jane Doe's picture from his pocket and held it up, comparing it to the deceased.

He handed it to me when he was finished. "What do you think?"

I bent down to get a better look at the victim. It was her, alright. She likely knew her killer. There appeared to be no defensive reaction or any attempt to flee the vehicle. I pictured her sitting there calmly, having a conversation when she got her brains blown out. I resisted the urge to draw my sidearm and put another hole in her head for Jenn. It took every ounce of restraint that I had. Ziggy tugged at my arm, no doubt sensing my distress.

I straightened up and nodded. "It's her."

The crime scene investigator arrived, followed by the coroner. Ziggy suggested I walk over to the bar next door to ask around, or perhaps to keep me out of the way.

The air inside smelled of stale cigarettes and beer, and I paused a moment for my eyes to adjust to the dim lighting. A handful of what appeared to be regulars hugged the long bar. A dozen or so empty tables were scattered around the remaining space.

I approached the bar where a large, bearded man wearing an apron around his waist loaded long-neck bottles into a cooler. He stopped when he noticed me.

"What can I do for you, Sheriff?"

I decided not to correct him. "Did you know a woman was shot in the parking lot next door?"

"I saw the commotion on the way in. Figured one of the regulars would tell me about it when they get here."

"Were you working last night?"

"All night, every night." He shook his tired head. "Hard to find good help anymore."

I handed him the victim's picture. "Recognize her?"

He studied it for a moment and nodded as he handed it back. "She was in here last night with some dude I'd never seen before."

"You sure it was her?"

He wiped his hands with a rag and set it on the bar. "I get pretty busy, so I don't pay much attention, but they got pretty loud. Thought I was gonna have to throw them out."

"What did the dude look like?"

He gave a broad description that could have been Finn or a hundred other guys. I wished I had thought to take a picture of Finn the last time I'd seen him.

I pulled the motel picture from my pocket and set it on the bar. "It wasn't him, was it?"

He picked it up. "No." He shook his head and handed me the photo. "This guy's too big."

"Do you remember when they left?"

"He dragged her out of here around midnight." He picked up something from the back counter and set it on the bar. "She left without her cell phone."

I held open an evidence bag and had him drop it in, then nodded my head toward the customers. "Mind if I ask around?"

"Knock yourself out."

The third man I asked thought he might have seen them leave around midnight, but given that he was on his second drink at three in the afternoon, I questioned his reliability.

Back at the crime scene, I told Ziggy she'd been in the bar last night with a man. Might have left around midnight. He didn't comment when I gave him the description, but I don't recall he'd ever gotten up close and personal with Finn.

I held up the evidence bag. "Found her phone."

"Good work." Ziggy's smile gave way to a serious expression. "Coroner said she took one shot from a nine millimeter. Estimated time of death was between ten and two last night. Said he could narrow it down after he got her back to the morgue."

"Find any ID?"

"Car's registered here in Park County to a Kayla Green. She's got a handful of priors, mostly misdemeanors."

Kayla Green appeared to be a loose end that someone decided needed to be tightened up. If it wasn't Finn doing the tightening, I had a feeling he might be next. One could only hope.

Ziggy gestured toward his car. "Let's go check out the address on her registration while we're out here."

We pulled up in front of the address ten minutes later.

"You sure this is it?"

He checked the paper again. "That's what it says here."

We stared out the window at an empty lot that hadn't seen a lawn mower in more than a couple of years.

CHAPTER THIRTEEN

I checked in with Jenn on the drive back to the station. She told me Maria was taking good care of her, and she felt safer knowing the Whitehawks were keeping an eye on the ranch. I told her I'd be home in an hour.

"All quiet on the western front," I said to Ziggy when I hung up.

"Let's hope it stays that way."

We were going to need more than hope.

Back at the office, I sat at my desk, one of three in an open area nicknamed the bullpen. Ziggy had a proper office with a door on the opposite side of the room. The desk had more drawers than I could fill in ten years. The previous occupant, which I guessed would have been Ziggy, had left some office supplies, evidence bags, zip ties, and a box of latex gloves.

Ziggy tossed me the bag containing Kayla's phone. "Why don't you see what you can find on this. When you're done, send it to the lab for prints."

I slipped on a pair of gloves and removed the phone from the bag—a prepaid phone with basic features, commonly referred to as a burner, used by people who prefer anonymity.

The call log contained about a dozen entries, most of them to the same number, shortly before and after the hospital incident. After recording all the numbers on my desktop computer, I dialed the most popular number—no answer and no voice-mail—probably another burner. I wrote the number in the little notepad that every good cop carried in his shirt pocket.

Kayla Green was a ghost. We had nothing—no family, friends, or neighbors to contact. I pulled her file up on the computer and copied the Arizona address she'd given at the time of her last arrest. Probably another empty lot.

I hadn't considered the moral dilemma that I might face when I agreed to take this job. The victim whose killer I was charged with bringing to justice was the same person who tried to put Jenn in the ground. Ordinarily, my *give-a-shit* meter would bottom out, but I wanted to prove my theory that Finn was involved.

After I signed the chain of custody form and secured the evidence, I said goodnight to Ziggy and headed home for dinner.

"Where's Jenn?" I asked Maria when I got home.

"She just went upstairs."

I lowered my voice. "Is she okay?"

"Oh, yes. We made dinner together. Breaded pork chops."

"Sounds like she had a good day."

"She got a call this afternoon that upset her, but other than that, yes, it was a good day."

"Do you know who called?"

"She didn't say."

"Hi, Dillon," Jenn said on her way down the stairs. "I didn't hear you come in."

"Hey, Babe. I heard you made dinner."

"Y'all heard right."

She sounded more like herself, and I smiled at her progress. I had a feeling we'd dodged a bullet.

Alex ran down the stairs and threw a hug around my waist. "Hey, Pop. Did you catch any bad guys today?"

"Not yet, but I will." I made a gun with my thumb and fore-finger. "You better behave yourself, or I'll have to take *you* in."

Maria's husband was working late that night, so I invited her to stay for dinner. After dinner, Alex played a video game in the living room while Jenn and I cleaned the kitchen. She washed, and I dried.

"Mort called today," Jenn said with her hands in the sink.

"What did he want?"

She dried her hands on a towel. "I think Finn tried to kill me."

"Mort told you that?"

"Not exactly. He said because I inherited this land, it's not considered marital property, so Finn would have no right to it in a divorce settlement."

I scratched the space above my lip. "Apparently, Finn's one step ahead of us. He must have known that when he tried to blackmail me."

Jenn tilted her head. "When? What did he say?"

"The night I saw him at the motel, he told me he would agree to a divorce and be out of our lives on one condition—you sign over his half of the ranch."

"His half? He doesn't own shit." She turned away, and I reached for her arm.

"I think somehow he knows that. That's why he wants the deed first. If you divorced him now, he'd be entitled to nothing."

She studied my face. "What did you tell him?"

"I told him to go shit in his hat... but I may have used stronger language."

"How did he take it?"

"Not much he could say. I had a gun to his head."

Jenn's eyes grew wide. "You went there with a gun?"

"No, it was his."

She shook her head like she was trying to wake herself from a bad dream.

I needed to redirect. "Did Mort say anything else?"

"He said I needed a will because if I were to die without one, Finn would get everything."

"That's why he tried to kill you."

"He said he could draft a will that specifically excludes Finn. The beneficiary could be a trust for Alex with you as trustee."

"You can do that? Exclude people, I mean."

"I'm telling you what he said. We need to get it done as soon as possible, and you need to let Finn know killing me will get him nothing."

I exhaled and felt some of the heaviness lifted from my shoulders. The will should neutralize the threat of Finn killing Jenn. We still had to figure out a way to get them unhitched without Jenn signing away half the ranch.

I looked at my phone. "It's getting late, and he's an hour later in Texas. I'll call him in the morning."

A few seconds passed. Jenn took a deep breath. "There's something else I wanted to talk to you about."

I braced myself. "What is it?"

"I think it's time to move forward with the riding center."

The Asha Whitehawk Equine Therapy Center, named after Uncle Roy's deceased fiancée and Jacob and Jeremiah's mother, was a promise Jenn had made to her uncle before he died. Uncle Roy had drawn up plans and willed his property to Jenn so she could make his dream a reality.

Roy and Asha loved horses, particularly those that previous owners had abused. They provided the love and care that had been missing in these animals' lives and envisioned a place where the animals could provide the same for individuals of all ages with cognitive, physical, emotional and learning disabilities.

Jenn grew up spending summers with Uncle Roy and his horses, so she became the logical choice to carry on his legacy. Unfortunately, there wasn't a lot of money to be made from rescuing horses, and the ranch had fallen on hard times. Roy had planned to sell off some of the land to finance his dream.

"You're going to need lots of money to get this thing off the ground."

"I've been thinking about selling some of the land."

"To Riverdale?"

"Absolutely not. There's a farmer who owns land that borders the ranch to the south. He's been trying to buy more from Uncle Roy for years. He wanted three hundred acres."

"That's half the ranch."

"What do I need it for? There'd be more than enough for the riding center."

"What's it worth?"

"Last I knew, he was offering fifteen hundred dollars an acre. Probably worth more now."

"Do you think he'll turn around and sell it to Riverdale for a profit?"

"That land's no good to Riverdale without mine." She paused, and a smile flickered on her lips. "I can't wait to see the look on Finn's face when he hears I sold half the ranch."

"Let me know when you tell him, so I can take a picture."

She smiled and nodded. "Know any good lawyers?"

Chapter Fourteen

Jenn pressed charges against Dallarosa, and Riverdale promptly bailed him out. One of their high-priced lawyers would no doubt swoop in and get him off, but Jenn said it was the principle. The man broke the law, violated her rights, and she couldn't let him get away without sleeping at least one night on a prison cot.

I called Mort and told him to draw up the will. He said he could have it done in a couple of days and email the documents for her to sign and get notarized. A little more weight had been lifted. I asked if there was any way she could divorce Finn without his signature. The short answer was no. He mentioned a default divorce, but that was only if the other spouse could not be found, and you could demonstrate that you'd made diligent or reasonable efforts to locate them through a process server. If served, he had twenty-eight days to respond.

I thought about the engagement ring hidden in the back of my sock drawer. It would have to stay there until Jenn got a proper divorce.

Monday night had come and gone. Finn did not show his face at the Riverdale meeting. My heart wanted to believe that he was out of our lives for good, but my head wouldn't let it.

The meeting ended in another free-for-all that took all three of us to break up. We didn't make any arrests. This was a small town where everybody knew everybody else. We let them off with a warning, even though it didn't look like anyone would be shaking hands and making up anytime soon.

The phone on my desk rang, and I picked it up.

"Dillon, y'all better get home right away. Finn just pulled up."

"On my way." I grabbed my hat and ran out the door.

I flipped on the lights and siren and made the fifteen-minute trip in seven. I tore up the drive and skidded to a stop in front of the house. Jenn and Finn stood next to a blue sedan. He had hold of her arm.

I jumped from the Bronco and didn't ask questions. Finn turned toward me, and I dropped him like a bag of hammers.

He shook his head to clear it and touched his nose. "I think you broke my nose," he said, looking up at me from the dirt.

My boot on his chest kept him down. "How many times do I have to tell you to leave us alone?"

He wiped a bloody lip with the back of his hand. "I'll see you in court for that."

"I don't think so." I glanced at Jenn, who appeared to be alright. "Jenn here will testify that a sheriff's deputy arrived as she was being assaulted and used an appropriate amount of force to subdue her attacker."

"Appropriate?"

I rested my hand on my sidearm. "I could have put a bullet in your head and been justified, given that Glock in your belt."

I took a step back and let him pull himself up. He took a moment to brush the dirt from his clothes. I turned him around, pulled the gun from his belt, and removed the clip. I tossed both into the back seat of his car.

"What are you doing here?"

"I came to finalize our deal. My buyer is getting impatient."

"You can forget about any deals," Jenn said through her teeth.

"Have you forgotten we're still married? No deal, no divorce."

"You tried to kill me."

He shifted his weight to the other foot. "I did no such thing."

"That's right, *you* didn't," I said. "You hired Kayla Green to do it."

I watched his reaction. He wore a decent poker face, but he shifted his weight again.

"I don't know who that is."

"Stop trying to kill me. It won't do you any good. I have a will excluding you from getting anything. The only thing killing me will get you is a prison sentence."

He pulled a handkerchief from his pocket and dabbed at the blood beneath his nose, his expression unreadable. His movements seemed ordinary and ominous at the same time.

"Well played," he said after a few moments of silence. "But this game is far from over."

I had a feeling he'd outmaneuvered us again.

"I hoped it wouldn't come to this, but you leave me no choice."

"What are you talking about?" Jenn had three speeds—off, on, and don't push your luck—and she was shifting into third.

I took a step closer to Jenn in case I had to restrain her. "Just spit it out."

"I think you may have already figured out that your adoption was illegal."

He thought wrong.

"Both spouses must agree to the action... and that didn't happen."

Jenn's eyes lit up like the afterburners on an F-16. I extended my arm in front of her.

"There are only a few people who know that we're still married. If you'd like to keep it that way, you'll need to sign over half of this land." He let his words hang there for a moment. "I would need the north half, of course. I already have a buyer lined up."

I felt Jenn push against my arm. "You sleazy son of the devil…"

"I hoped this could be a bit more amicable."

"To think I was actually considering paying you to go away." She snorted. "Not anymore. Y'all ain't getting one dime from me."

"I'm sure they'll be able to find a decent home for the boy."

"His name is Alex and—"

"Let's take a breath." I pulled her aside. Unfortunately, the law was on his side. "Maybe we should investigate a financial solution?"

"You should listen to your boyfriend."

"Shut your pie hole."

I placed my hands on her shoulders. "That's not helping."

"Don't you see why that won't work?" She slipped from my grasp and took a step backward. "Every time he gets himself in trouble, and I can guarantee this won't be the last, he's going to show up here looking for another handout."

She knew him better than I did, and I reckoned she was right.

I turned to him. "These people who want to kill you… how much do you owe them?"

"Twenty grand, give or take."

"What if I were to cover your debt?"

"Dillon!"

"That's very generous, but half of this ranch is worth a lot more than that." A crooked smile snaked across his lips. "What kind of businessman would I be if I made a deal like that?"

"A live one."

Finn shook his head. "Where are all the witnesses when you need them?"

"You don't have a legal leg to stand on. Jenn inherited this land. You have no claim to it, married or otherwise. You get an easy twenty grand for signing divorce papers and never bothering us again. I'd say that's a good deal."

"I disagree."

"I'll have the papers drawn up."

"Let's not get ahead of ourselves." He walked toward his car, a different model than the last time he was here. He probably switched them out every few days.

Jenn took a couple of steps toward him, and I followed. I pulled my phone out, opened the camera app, and tucked it behind my back. I needed his picture.

"Finn? What are you going to do?" She stopped to wait for his answer.

When he turned, I snapped a picture from my hip.

"You'll be the first to know," he said, unaware of the photo, and drove away.

"Where would you get that kind of money?" Jenn asked me as he drove off.

"I'll figure something out." I glanced around the property. "Time to circle the wagons. Alex is going to have to stay out of school for a while. We need to assume that Finn is coming after him."

"What if he turns us in, and CPS shows up to take Alex away?"

"I'll talk to the Whitehawks. Nobody gets past the front gate. I'll check in with Mort in the meantime."

"Dillon, do you really think he would rat me out like that?"

"If you're asking if I think he's capable of doing it, I'd say yes. But Big Ugly Guy from the motel might force him to reconsider our offer."

"What are you talking about?"

I pulled the motel picture from my pocket and handed it to her. "This guy."

She studied it. "Who is it?"

"The motel owner told me he was looking for Finn before I got there. Probably the guy he owes money to."

She snorted. "Maybe you should help this guy find him."

I said nothing.

"Isn't there something you can do?"

"Dead men don't talk."

"What does that mean?"

"I'm afraid we'll never be rid of Finn Rafferty until he's dead." I paused. "Even if I arrested him for blackmail, I can't trust that justice will be served. Remember what happened back in Texas?"

I took Jenn's lack of response as silent agreement.

"I can talk to Mort," I said.

Her shoulders fell. "Maybe I should just give him what he wants. I'll sell the rest, and we can all move back to Texas."

The part about moving didn't seem like such a bad idea. But I wasn't about to be bullied by the likes of Finn Rafferty.

"You don't mean that." I put my arm around her shoulders. "Why don't you go inside and relax for a while?"

"Seriously? I can't relax right now."

"Where's Maria?"

"I told her to stay inside."

"I don't think Finn will be back today. Maybe you can have Maria fix you a drink to relax."

She folded her arms across her chest. "I'm perfectly capable of fixing my own drink." She let her arms fall to her side and her expression softened. "Come with me?"

I shrugged. "Sorry, Babe, but I have to get back to work."

"Y'all better tell Ziggy what's going on."

I nodded, gave her a kiss, and sent her back into the house. Ziggy was on a need-to-know basis, and at this point, he didn't need to know.

Buck had been watching from the barn and walked toward me. "Did I hear her say something about selling the ranch?"

I wasn't about to mention her remark about moving. That was desperation talking. "She's thinking about selling off some land to finance the riding center that Roy wanted to build."

"To Riverdale?"

"No."

"Okay, then." He took a pinch of tobacco from a round tin and placed it between his cheek and gum. "A bunch of us is gettin' together tonight to figure out how we can keep that damn casino from bein' built. Wanna tag along?"

I tapped the badge on my chest. "I should probably stay neutral. Besides, I'm on call tonight."

"Well, in case you change your mind, we'll be at Hank Coleman's place up the road. It's the big red barn on the right."

I nodded. There were probably five big red barns on the right between here and town. "Don't do anything stupid."

"We're just talkin'."

I studied him as he spat a stream of tobacco juice into the dirt. He made the meeting sound like a social event. I knew better. "Have you seen the Whitehawks? I'm paying them to provide security, and Finn just waltzed through the front gate."

"You know, there's only two of them and about six hundred acres. On top a that, one works days and the other nights."

First time I'd ever heard Buck stick up for the brothers, but he was right. I needed more security. "Got any ideas?"

"I know some other fellas who might be interested. Them Whitehawks probably have some relations that could help, too."

"Okay. You're in charge of Human Resources. We need a half dozen more bodies."

"I'll get right on it."

"And make sure someone is watching the gate."

That's when I remembered the two security cameras that Coop set up last year in the barn. They were in the house somewhere. Setting them up to watch the perimeter of the house sounded like a good idea.

"What was Rafferty doing here, anyway?" Buck asked.

I figured Buck ought to know, so I didn't sugarcoat it. "Blackmailing Jenn."

His mustache twitched. "Damn it, sonny. You're the law now."

He had a point.

"Why didn't you lock him up?"

I shrugged. "I'm new at this. I didn't think about it like that."

"Blackmail, huh?"

"Yeah. He wants half the ranch, or he's going to have Alex taken away."

He turned his head and spat another stream of tobacco juice. "What's the boy got to do with anything?"

"Turns out Jenn is still married to that asshat, Rafferty. Long story short, Alex's adoption didn't take because Finn never signed off. He's threatening to tell the authorities."

Buck's eyes locked onto mine. "Want me to kill the son of a bitch?"

That would be great. I paused. "No, Buck. I definitely do not want you to kill him."

"Look, I'm an old man. I ain't got much to live for. That boy belongs here with you and Jenny."

"I agree Alex belongs with us, but there's gotta be another way."

"I seen his type before." Buck frowned and shook his head. "He won't stop until he gets what he wants."

Chapter Fifteen

I called Mort on the way back to the station.

"So, what can we do about this Finn thing?"

"The will that I'm working on should take care of any death threats."

"So you don't think he'll try to kill her again once he knows about the will?"

"What? He tried to kill her?"

"A woman posing as a nurse tried to kill her while she was in the hospital. I think Finn hired her. Then he killed her to cover his tracks."

"Is Jenn alright?"

"She's fine now, but she gave us all a scare."

"Besides a will, I'm afraid she'll need a restraining order."

I blew out a breath. "This guy is getting to be a real pain in my ass."

"Dillon, don't do anything stupid."

I'd told Buck the same thing less than an hour ago, but I wasn't sure either of us would listen. "Now, Finn's threatening to have Alex taken away because the adoption was illegal."

"Unfortunately, he's right. Consent of both spouses is necessary for a valid adoption to take place. In the absence of awareness and consent of one, the adoption would be considered void. There's really nothing you can do to protect Alex."

"But she can adopt him if they get divorced, right?"

"That's correct. She could reapply once she's single again."

"He says he won't agree to a divorce until after she signs over half the ranch." I exhaled. "It sounds like this could go on forever and a day."

"I wish I had better news."

Me, too. I thought Mort would pull a rabbit out of his hat and make this all go away. I reckoned it was on me now.

The rest of the day dragged. I handled a call about some stolen chickens, but everything seemed so inconsequential compared to our situation. I told the owner if he ever called 911 again about a chicken, I would arrest him.

When I got back to the station, the report from Kayla's phone was on my desk. They'd lifted a partial print that did not belong to Kayla, but not enough to attempt a match. Another dead end.

I stopped on the way out to say goodnight to Ziggy.

"The phone was a bust."

He looked up from his desk. "I saw that." He studied me for a moment. "You look like you could use a drink."

"More than one, I'm afraid." I almost left it at that, but Jenn would ask me tonight if I'd told Ziggy about Finn's visit, and I didn't want to suffer her wrath if I said no. "Finn stopped by the house today."

Ziggy leaned back in his chair and motioned for me to have a seat. "How did that go?"

I think I broke his nose. "Not good. He's got us over a barrel, and I don't know what to do about it."

I explained our situation and today's threat escalation. "I don't think he'll try to kill her again, but I'm worried that he'll tear our family apart if Jenn doesn't give in to his demands."

"I wish there was something I could say that would help, but unless we can prove he committed a crime, there's really nothing we can do. And putting aside the Kayla murder for a moment, he hasn't committed any crimes that I can tell."

"I need to stop him. I know he killed Kayla, I just can't prove it... yet."

"Whatever you need..."

"Thanks."

"Now go home and have that drink." He smiled. "Have one for me, too."

"I'm on call tonight."

He winced. "I'll only call if it's an emergency."

"Stolen chickens don't constitute an emergency, right?"

"I guess it depends on whose chickens." He smiled and waved me off.

***

Jenn met me at the door when I got home. "If you're dragging anything home from work, y'all need to go back outside and leave it on the porch."

"Do I look that bad?" I glanced in the mirror near the door, then scanned the room. "Where is everybody?"

"I sent Maria home, and Alex is upstairs."

"What's going on?"

"We're taking a break. It's only for one night. We can do that, can't we?"

"Depends on what you mean by a break." I waited with a raised brow.

"I mean we're not even going to think about anything nega-tive. The three of us are going to have a nice family dinner and talk about positive things."

I pull her in for a hug. "I think I can handle that."

We lingered there for a moment.

She leaned back and a touch of the sparkle that had been missing from those beautiful blue eyes returned. "Y'all think you can keep that thing holstered until Alex goes to bed?"

"It's been in there so long, I reckon I can wait a couple more hours." I liked where this night was headed.

Jenn had thawed some steaks, which I grilled on the back deck, and the three of us had a nice family dinner despite the elephant in the room. Just for a moment, I wondered if this might be our last big meal together. Jenn caught my stare, and her eyes told me she wondered the same.

After dinner, we settled in for movie night. Alex chose *Mrs. Doubtfire*, where Robin Williams plays a recently divorced actor who dresses up as a female housekeeper to be able to interact with his kids. We had a lot of laughs, despite the serious subject matter. Alex had no way of knowing how prophetic the premise might be.

I pushed that thought aside. "Who wants popcorn?"

The vote was unanimous.

Alex fell asleep just before the end of the movie, and I carried him up to bed. Jenn followed a few minutes later and brushed by me in the hall with a seductive look.

We made love with a silent intensity, each needing some-thing from the other that had been missing since before Jenn's accident. After Jenn fell peacefully asleep, I extracted myself from a tangle of arms, legs and cotton sheets. I lay on my back, still feeling the glow.

The digital clock in the bedroom projected the time on the ceiling in big red numbers. I watched those numbers change as

I listened to Jenn's slow rhythmic breath, feeling more relaxed than I'd been since I could remember. She was right. We needed a break from the turmoil that had threatened to drive a wedge between us, and I vowed to never let that happen.

While Jenn's secrets had contributed to our setback, I applauded her initiative in getting us back on track. Why had I been so unwilling, or unable, to make such a move? It wasn't a conscious thing. Perhaps I was more like Pop than I cared to admit. I attempted to push that thought aside as I drifted off to sleep.

My phone rang on the nightstand, shattering an otherwise peaceful sleep. At first, I had trouble making sense of the numbers on the ceiling. My brain eventually arranged them to read twelve thirty-four. It took another ring before I moved my arms.

"Sorry to call so late," Ziggy said, "but I need you."

"What's the matter?" I glanced at Jenn, who hadn't moved.

"Meet me at Hank Coleman's place. You can't miss it. It's the one with the big fireball."

Hank Coleman? Buck was there tonight. "On my way."

Chapter Sixteen

I saw Buck's truck heading for the front gate as I jumped off the porch and ran toward the Bronco. I flagged him down, and he rolled down his window.

"Where are you going?"

"Hank Coleman's barn is on fire."

"They won't let you get anywhere near there. Turn around and go back to bed."

"The hell I will."

I glared at him for a moment, knowing I wouldn't be able to change his mind. "You can ride with me."

"Thanks," he said when he climbed into the passenger seat. "I still got that bum tire."

"How'd you hear about the fire?"

"Hank called everyone that was there tonight to warn them."

"Warn them about what?"

"That we might be next."

I flipped on the lights and siren when we reached the road. "So you think someone's after you because you're organizing against the casino?"

He looked at me, and I caught his stare. "I don't think. I know."

"Do you have any proof?"

"Not yet."

"You need to let the sheriff's department handle this. I don't want to see you get hurt."

The sky lit up orange when we rounded the bend before Hank's place.

"Holy horseshit!"

"If Riverdale is behind this," I said. "They're not messing around. You need to be careful."

I turned in the drive and pulled up alongside Ziggy's empty vehicle.

"You stay here," I said.

"The hell I—"

"Alright." I held up a hand. "Just stay out of the way."

Flames fully engulfed the barn, and a wall of hot air greeted us as we left the relative safety of the Bronco. Hot ash rained down around us, threatening the Coleman house. Two fire companies had already responded, but the intense heat kept them at bay. A third company arrived right behind us and set up near the house.

I noticed Ziggy talking to Hank at the edge of the fray. He looked at me with a *what's-he-doing-here* look when he saw Buck. I shrugged. Hank nodded toward us before continuing his conversation.

"It's them Riverdale jackals," Hank said. "They want our land, and they don't care how they get it."

Ziggy held up his hands. "Hank, we don't know if this was arson, or something else."

"C'mon, Sheriff. A barn full of hay doesn't go up that quickly without some help."

I interrupted. "You had a meeting here tonight to brainstorm how to stop the casino, didn't you?"

Hank glared at me, and then Buck.

"Who else knew about it?"

"Just the attendees... and apparently you." He sent another glare Buck's way.

"For starters," Ziggy said, "I'm going to need a list of everyone who was here, and anyone who was invited but didn't show."

"Everyone showed. They're all good people. None of them would ever think of doing something like this."

"That may be, but I still need the list."

Everyone took a moment.

"Any animals involved?" Ziggy asked.

"No, thank the Lord." He pointed to another building farther up the drive. "The horses are all in the stables over yonder."

"Anything in the barn besides hay?"

"A tractor, my workshop, and a meetin' area I set up for our group. All of tonight's work was in there."

We all watched a group of firefighters struggle to knock down the flames that shot up through a large hole in the roof. Hank's tear-filled eyes reflected the ghastly orange glow.

Hank punched a fist into an open hand. "By God, someone's gonna pay for this."

Ziggy put a hand on his shoulder. "We're going to find out what happened."

When Hank excused himself to go check on the horses, I pulled the picture of Finn's map up on my phone and showed it to Ziggy.

"Where'd you get that?"

"Finn had it." I didn't wait for a comment. "Do you think he's trying to... facilitate these deals?"

"It didn't make sense until I saw that map." Ziggy frowned. "There's been a rash of fires, equipment mishaps, and sick horses over the past few months. At first it seemed like a random streak of bad luck, but they've all taken place in the highlighted areas of that map."

"So, you think Riverdale is squeezing out these smaller ranchers?"

"Some of these people are just getting by. They don't have the money to rebuild a barn, or buy more hay, or lose any animals. They'd be forced to sell."

"I reckon they brought out the big guns for Jenn," I said. "If I'm reading this map right, her land is the linchpin that holds this deal together."

"At first, I wasn't too thrilled about you hiring the White-hawks, but I suppose it's a good thing they'll be right there at the ranch."

Buck joined us.

I looked at both of them. "I'm tellin' you, Finn is somehow involved in all this."

"You have evidence to back that up?"

"Yes... and no."

Ziggy arched an eyebrow. "Which is it?"

"I've seen it, but I don't have it. When I broke—uh, visit-ed—Finn's motel room, I saw emails and other communica-tions between Finn and Riverdale."

"We need to get them," Buck said.

Ziggy frowned, lost in thought, then turned to me. "Do you remember any names?"

I shook my head. "I was in a hurry. When I found the surveillance photos, I lost interest in the emails."

"Hey, Sheriff, did you ever find out who took them pho-tos?"

"Not yet." He glanced sideways at me, then looked at Buck. "Those photos were obtained illegally, so we can't use them as evidence."

"But they're still worth somethin' to us. Just like them emails would be if we had the names."

"That's true, but I can't condone the methods that were used to obtain those photos." He turned to me and held my gaze. "Do we all understand that?"

Buck and I nodded.

"Good. The fire investigators will be here in the morning. Why don't you go home and get some sleep? We'll set up some interviews tomorrow when I get Hank's list."

"I can tell you who was there," Buck offered.

"You mind coming into the station tomorrow and giving a statement?"

"Anything I can do to help, Sheriff."

Buck broke the silence on the way back to the ranch. "So, what are you going to do about this?"

"Well, while we're waiting for the fire investigator's report, we'll interview Hank and anyone who was there tonight."

"I'll tell you what's on that report. A-R-S-O-N."

"I think maybe we'll wait for the official report."

"An' what about Rafferty? You gonna interview *him*?"

"Sure, once we find him."

"Are ya lookin'?" He didn't wait for a reply. "What about them emails?"

"When we find Finn, we'll get a warrant."

"IF ya find him."

I gave Buck a sideways glance but said nothing.

"Them Whitehawk boys could find him. Why don't you hire them?"

"They've already got a job. Anyway, that's not how the sheriff's department operates."

"Well, maybe it should." He pulled at his mustache. "You're lucky I'm still around to be havin' this conversation. All us folks coulda been on the menu at that barbecue tonight. Someone's gonna get hurt if we don't do somethin' quick."

Chapter Seventeen

I dragged myself out of bed the next morning and inhaled two cups of coffee. Jenn hadn't heard me leave last night, but she woke when I returned, and we talked for half an hour. She fell back to sleep. I wasn't so lucky.

Some of the tension that had built up between us was released last night, like opening a safety valve on a runaway boiler. Enjoyable as it was, I hoped we could get back to a routine that didn't need to rely on safety-valve sex.

We had taken a break last night from the drama, but today was a new day and the clock had not stopped ticking. Any minute, a process server, a CPS investigator, or a hired gunman could knock on our front door. I needed to keep any of that from happening.

Since we'd taken Alex out of school until this mess blew over, I didn't need to walk him to the bus stop, so I headed to the office early. A smoldering pile of rubble covered the ground where Hank Coleman's barn used to be. The fire investigators appeared to be on site. Hank had been wronged, and someone should have to pay. I wanted that someone to be Finn, whether he did this or not. I made a mental note to ask Mort if Jenn could get some kind of default divorce if Finn went to prison.

I didn't trust law enforcement or the legal system. Sounds funny coming from a sheriff's deputy, but after what I'd been through with Luke and my daddy in Texas, I had serious reservations. Maybe I took this job to prove that an honest man can survive in the system. I'd only been on the job for a week, so that remained to be seen.

Even if Finn went to prison, that wouldn't solve all of our problems. If he opened his mouth about the illegal adoption before Jenn could get a divorce, we could lose Alex. *Dead men tell no tales.* I immediately felt Luke's presence in the vehicle reminding me that crossing that line would only make me part of the corrupt system that I despised.

I couldn't shake the thought that, while Mort was working on a plan to keep Alex at home with us, Finn was holed up somewhere working on a plan to take him away. We were running out of options, and I would not stand by and watch that happen.

The first step was to find him. I had the make and color of his rental car, but I'd been so distracted that I'd failed to get the plate number. I could probably get a long list of matches from DMV, but by the time I narrowed it down, he'd be gone. Finn had become a moving target after I chased him out of Redfield. I needed to think like him and figure out his next move before he did.

Ziggy and I spent the rest of that day and most of the next interviewing the eleven people who'd attended the meeting at Hank Coleman's place the night of the fire.

Everyone gave similar answers to our questions. I didn't get the feeling they were hiding anything, until we got to Joe Dunning, who owned a small ranch in the path of Riverdale's expansion plans. He arrived late Friday afternoon, our last interview.

I'd been a little too eager to pin this on Finn during a few of the other interviews, so Ziggy suggested that I *observe*—a polite way of telling me to keep my mouth shut. I was allowed in the room with him but not allowed to speak.

"Did anyone outside the group know about the meeting?" Ziggy asked.

Joe hesitated. "No."

"You don't sound too sure."

More hesitation. "The group was sworn to secrecy. Hank said we could be in danger and asked if anyone would like to leave before we got started. No one took him up on his offer."

"So, Hank wasn't surprised when his barn burned down a couple hours after your meeting broke up?"

"I'd say he was relieved that it didn't burn while we were still in it."

"Why put yourselves in harm's way?"

"None of us wants to leave, Sheriff." He shook his head. "And none of us wants this casino in our backyard if we stay."

Ziggy paused. "So, who else knew?"

"Like I said, we were pretty tight-lipped about the meeting, figuring something like this might happen."

"But you told someone, didn't you?"

Joe shuffled his feet and straightened in his chair. "Just that fella from the BLM."

"BLM?" I asked.

Ziggy glanced at me. "Bureau of Land Management."

"What was I supposed to do?" More feet shuffling. "He said he was on our side. Said he came to town to protect folks like us that opposed the casino, and that I couldn't tell anyone about our conversation."

"Did you? Tell anyone?"

"No, sir."

I wanted to jump in, but I held back.

"How did you know he was a BLM agent?"

"He flashed a badge when we first met."

"What was his name?"

Joe shrugged. "It happened so fast, I didn't have time to read it. He might have said Fletcher or something like that."

I couldn't take it any longer. "Do you think you would recognize him if you saw him again?"

"I think so."

I felt Ziggy's glare as I pulled out my phone and showed Finn's photo to Joe. "Is that the BLM agent?"

He nodded. "That's him."

I shot Ziggy an *I-told-you-so* look. He shrugged.

"So you guys know him?"

"Do you know how to get in touch with him," I asked.

"No, sir. He just showed up at my house on Monday."

"What kind of car did he drive?"

His eyes darted back and forth under a furrowed brow. After a few seconds, he gave a quick nod. "It was a Toyota. A green one."

We thanked him for his honesty and assured him we would keep this conversation confidential."

After he left, Ziggy called me into his office. Even though I had gotten some useful information and a solid ID, I didn't think I'd been summoned for a pat on the back.

"Before you say anything," Ziggy said. "I want to remind you that you're off this weekend."

A part-time deputy named Ferguson held down the fort on the weekends with Ziggy and me taking turns with on-call duty.

Ziggy knew I couldn't sit on this new information for two days. However, I had a couple of important things to do this weekend that would take up some of my time. Mort had sent

Jenn's will earlier in the day, so we needed time to read it over and have Hattie notarize it as soon as possible.

I also needed to spend some quality time with the family. Jenn and I had turned a corner Tuesday night along a road that, in retrospect, had been headed for a cliff. I couldn't let that happen. Tomorrow night I planned to take the family to the Bluebird Restaurant to help keep us from turning back.

"Dillon?"

"Yes, sir?"

"Ferg will be here all weekend. I don't want to hear that you were anywhere near the station. Got it?"

What I heard was, *whatever you do this weekend is unofficial business. Keep your uniform in your closet and don't do anything too stupid.* "Roger that."

CHAPTER EIGHTEEN

Jenn's will, which excluded Finn Rafferty from even one dime of her estate, became official as of ten thirty Saturday morning. Raven and I witnessed the document that Hattie notarized as Alex played his handheld video game in an adjoining room. While it was a huge step in the right direction and should eliminate the threat of Finn killing her to get the ranch, it did nothing to stop him from tearing Alex away from us.

The pressure I was under to keep that from happening would have kept me up at night if not for Leotie's rain dance tea, which I'd nearly used up over the past two weeks.

On our way home, I told Alex and Jenn about my plans to take them out to the Bluebird for dinner. A gorgeous smile from Jenn and a fist bump from Alex told me I'd made the right decision.

Jenn's phone rang, and she quickly dismissed the call.

"Who was that?"

"Wrong number."

"Really?" I turned to her. "How do you know that? You didn't answer it."

She hesitated. "I just know."

"C'mon, Jenn. You can tell me."

More hesitation. "It's Finn, but it might as well be a wrong number because I'm never going to answer again."

I pulled the car off the road and skidded to a stop.

"Dillon!"

"I need to see your phone."

"Why?"

"Police business."

She squinted one eye and studied me with the other, then slapped her phone into my waiting hand.

I pulled out my notepad and compared the numbers. "Gotcha!"

"Got who?"

I held up the phone. "This number was all over Kayla's phone."

"Kayla?"

"The girl who tried to kill you."

"In other words, Finn tried to kill me?"

"When I find that snake, I'm going to kick his sorry ass all the way to Montana."

Jenn stared out the window and said nothing.

After I dropped them off, I headed to the Cheyenne village to find Cassidy.

"What's this?" Cassidy asked when I set the small cloth sack that Leotie had given me on the counter.

"It's a custom blend of tea given to me by a Cherokee medicine woman in Texas. I replaced some pretty strong PTSD medications with that tea."

She raised an eyebrow over a curious smile. "A medicine woman? I'm impressed." She looked inside the bag. "What do you want me to do with it?"

"Can you figure out what's in it and make some more?"

"I'm flattered that you think I can do the work of a medicine woman, but I don't have the knowledge or connection with Spirit that she does."

"Do you know someone who can do this? I'll pay them."

A customer approached the counter, and Cassidy excused herself. She returned a few minutes later.

"First, no true medicine woman would take your money. Second, I'm sure she knew exactly how much you needed. You must have faith."

Not what I wanted to hear. Faith seemed to disappear when you needed it the most.

She grabbed my wrist and turned it over to expose my tattoo. "You have marked yourself with the sign of the wolf. Do you know what that means?"

I hesitated, like it was a test. "At the time, I felt like a lone wolf, driven from the pack. I guess I needed to identify with something."

"The wolf is your spirit animal."

"Leotie told me that."

"The medicine woman?"

I nodded.

"That's what you needed then. Do you still need it?"

I shrugged. "I guess I don't anymore."

"What do you need now?"

Another shrug. "I was hoping *you* could tell *me*."

She looked into my eyes. "Do not look to others when the answer is within."

"I was afraid you were going to say something like that."

"The wolf is not afraid. He has a strong connection with instinct and intuition. The wolf is considered a medicine being associated with courage, strength, loyalty, and success at hunting. Perhaps this is what you need."

I smiled. "Yes. All the above."

"I cannot help you."

"Leotie said that, too." I now know why she said it. No one can help me but me.

She held up my cloth sack with a smile on her face. "You'll need the rest of this."

"Thank you."

"May the warm winds of Heaven blow softly upon you, and may the rainbow always touch your shoulder."

I left her café with a tip of my hat, disappointed but hopeful that she was right. I didn't get what I wanted, but I might have gotten what I needed.

On my way back to town, my stomach let me know that I'd forgotten to eat lunch. Around two thirty, I stopped at a little diner at the edge of town and sat in one of the booths with a view of the parking lot. I'd learned never to sit with my back to the door or windows.

Most places in town would comp a meal to men in uniform, but I'd promised Ziggy not to involve the department in my off-the-books investigation activities this weekend. I didn't know the owner well enough yet for him to recognize me as the new deputy in town without my uniform.

I had dinner plans with the family, so I ordered light—a sandwich and a cup of coffee. Halfway through my BLT, a car pulled into the lot. I couldn't see the driver through the tinted glass. He sat in his car, as if waiting for someone or something. Eventually, he stepped out into the sunlight. Big Ugly Guy from the motel scanned the parking lot before walking toward the front door.

I didn't recall ever meeting him, so I felt confident he didn't know who I was. He stepped inside, scanned the room, and walked toward my table. His picture didn't do him justice—he was bigger and uglier. He had a face like the back end of bad luck. His pockmarked skin looked like someone used his face for target practice, and his nose had been broken more than once. The nasty scar under his left eye completed the look.

The half-sandwich I'd just eaten nearly made another appearance when he slid into the booth across from me.

I pushed my plate toward him. "Wanna finish this? I just lost my appetite."

"You Dillon?"

"I am." I gave him a hard glare. "What do you want?"

He rested his forearms on the table. "I want you to tell me where I can find Finn Rafferty."

"I can't do that."

"Why not?"

"I don't know where he is."

"But you're looking for him."

"I imagine a lot of people are. What do you want him for?"

"Will you help me or not?"

I took a sip of lukewarm coffee. "I told you, I don't know where he is."

He removed one hand from the table. I thought he might have a gun, or he might reach under the table and rip one of my legs off.

The waitress walked by, and I raised my hand. "Check, please."

Big Ugly Guy frowned. "What's your rush. You got a date?"

"As a matter of fact, I do."

The waitress returned with the bill.

I picked up the check and studied it. "How much tip do you leave on a nine-dollar check?"

This was a scary dude, so I wasn't sure where my flippant attitude came from. Perhaps it had something to do with my recent chat with Cassidy. *The wolf is not afraid.*

Big Ugly Guy stood. "Just remember, I asked nicely." His steely eyes held my gaze. "The next time I won't be asking."

He left the diner. When he reached his car, he turned and saw me watching through the window. He pointed with two fingers at his eyes, then at me.

CHAPTER NINETEEN

I f my meeting with Big Ugly Guy was meant to rattle me, it worked. He knew my name, and he knew that I knew Finn, so he'd clearly been following me for some time.

I didn't want to mention any of this to Jenn, at least not yet. So, I would have to put it out of my mind for this evening. But before I could do that, I had to have a talk with the Whitehawks about a possible new threat.

I pulled up in front of the cabins and saw Jeremiah sitting on the front porch. I told him about Big Ugly Guy, and that we'd be away from home this evening, so everyone should be on high alert for anything unusual happening around the ranch.

"Pop's home," Alex called when I walked in the door at four thirty. He wore a pair of khakis and his favorite western shirt.

Jenn walked down the stairs looking pretty as a picture. "I thought you were gonna be home an hour ago."

"Me too, but something came up."

"Is everything all right?"

For now. "We're goin' out tonight. I'd say everything is just fine."

"Y'all better get changed. Alex is getting hungry."

I put on some clean clothes, and we piled into the Silverado.

The Bluebird Restaurant, about five miles south of Redfield in the middle of nowhere, did a bang-up business with their all-you-can-eat buffet on Saturday nights. We had to wait to be seated, which apparently was my fault for coming home late.

The first time we brought Alex here, he couldn't believe the variety of food, and that you could eat as much as you wanted. I reckoned the Bluebird lost money on at least one eleven-year-old boy that night. After teaching him how to pace himself to leave room for dessert, I introduced the young man to Oreo pie with a scoop of cookies 'n' cream ice cream on top.

We had a well-deserved night out as a family and agreed to do it more often. I glanced at Alex sitting between us on the way home and prayed that Finn Rafferty wouldn't stop that from happening.

We rounded a bend about two miles from home to find a large black sedan parked across the road in the twilight. I slammed on the brakes to keep from hitting it.

"Is everyone okay?"

Alex and Jenn nodded.

A man I'd never seen before climbed out of the driver's side and pointed a gun at me through the windshield. I had my backup piece strapped to my ankle, but I didn't want to put Jenn and Alex in the line of fire.

I threw the truck in reverse and glanced in the rearview just in time to see an SUV skid to a stop behind us. By this time, the gunman had reached the truck and opened my door.

"Get out."

His lips puckered up like a fish when he spoke. I told Jenn to stay inside, and I stepped out, the barrel of his gun leveled at my head.

"What do you want?"

"Shut up and put your hands against the car."

Given my military training, I had a better-than-average chance of disarming him and putting him on the ground before he could get a shot off. But I couldn't risk it with Jenn and Alex three feet away. Besides, there were two of them now.

I did as he asked. He patted me down and removed my gun and cell phone. As he zip-tied my hands behind my back, I watched Big Ugly Guy climb out of the SUV and walk to the passenger side of my truck.

"Leave her out of this."

He opened the door. "Get out."

I couldn't make out what Jenn said, but I didn't like the way she said it. "Just do what he says."

She emerged from the truck with Alex close behind.

"Cell phone," he said.

She slapped it into his hand, and he tossed it inside the truck. Fishlips did the same with my gun and phone.

"Where are you taking them?" I asked as he walked them toward the SUV.

"I warned you the last time we met." He pushed Jenn and Alex into the back seat. "This is me not asking."

Fishlips grabbed my arm and pulled me toward the sedan. I was stronger than him, but he had the gun.

"You better not hurt them," I shouted just before he pushed me into the trunk.

I'd never ridden inside a car trunk before. I wouldn't recommend it.

The car took a hard left, which told me we were headed south toward Cripple Creek. We drove for about fifteen minutes before asphalt turned to gravel and the car skidded to a stop.

"We'll switch seats on the way back," I said when he opened the trunk.

The business end of his Beretta M9 told me the answer was a hard no. He threw a burlap sack over my head and led me into a building. He removed the sack inside what appeared to be in an old construction trailer, turned on a lamp, and told me to sit. A desk, three chairs, and a pile of cardboard boxes were covered in a year's worth of dust.

He pointed to one of the chairs with his gun. "Sit."

He zip-tied my feet to the chair legs, then sat and waited. I'd never seen him before. His shaved head and thick beard made him look like his head was on upside down. The ink on his neck looked like a prison tat.

A half hour passed before Big Ugly Guy walked through the door.

"What have you done with Jenn and Alex?"

"They're safe... for now."

"You better not hurt them."

"That will depend on you."

He dismissed Fishlips, then pulled up a chair. "I don't feel like we finished our conversation at the diner."

"Do you have a name," I asked, "or should I just call you Big Ugly Guy?"

He hesitated. "My name is Vincent."

"Vincent? Not Vince or Vinnie or Sasquatch?"

"I prefer Vincent."

"You know I'm a deputy, right?"

"I know who you are and what you do."

"What do you want Rafferty for?"

"He owes some people some money."

"That's right. About twenty grand, if I recall." I shook my head. "I tried to give him the money to pay you back, but he refused to take it."

Vincent stared at me through squinted eyes, unsure whether to take me seriously.

"Looks like we're on the same side, Vincent."

"What are you talking about?"

"Let's say Finn doesn't have the money. What are you going to do?"

His eyes squinted again as he studied me.

"Are you going to kill him?"

"If I was, I wouldn't tell the sheriff. You think I'm stupid?"

I'm only the deputy, and yes. "Of course not. It's just that"—cover your ears, Luke—"I want him dead, too."

"What for?"

"He's still married to my girlfriend, and he's blackmailing her."

Vincent tilted his head and frowned. "I've never heard that one before."

My patience was wearing thin. "I'd love to explain it sometime over a couple of beers, but right now, I need to get back to Jenn and Alex."

He wagged his gun at me. "You're not going anywhere until you tell me where Finn Rafferty is."

If I knew, I'd tell him in a heartbeat. That would solve both of our problems. "I told you, I don't know where he is."

He folded his beefy arms across his chest. "I've got all night."

"Believe me, if I knew, I'd tell you."

"The sheriff's department is looking for him. You work for them. I need to find him first."

"The operative word there is *looking*. We haven't found him yet."

He stood. "Then we have a problem."

I tried to wrestle my arms free. The chair shook and the plastic ties cut into my wrists. "If anything happens to my family, I'll kill you."

This appeared to amuse him. "You're in no position to be threatening anyone, Sheriff." He stood. "I'll be back in a little while."

"It's Deputy," I shouted after he left.

Chapter Twenty

My attempts to free myself only resulted in a toppled chair and a nasty bump on my head. I thought about Jenn as I lay there helpless on the floor. I'd put her in harm's way again. She'd told me more than a dozen times that she's a big girl and she can take care of herself. But if I continued to bring trouble to her doorstep, something would eventually have to give.

I had no choice but to work with Vincent. Ironically, we both wanted the same thing. Given Finn's inability to pay off his creditors, it appeared that Vinnie and his boss wanted to kill him, perhaps to set an example. A cold Finn Rafferty on a slab in the morgue was at the top of my wish list, as well.

The door opened, and Vincent stepped inside.

"Is Jenn alright?" I asked from the floor.

He reached down with one hand and righted the chair. "That depends. Are you going to help me?"

"Either she's alright, or she isn't. Which is it?"

He hesitated, presumably to make me sweat a little more. "She's fine. That's not where I went."

I exhaled the breath I'd been holding. "Where did you go?"

"I wanted to give you some time alone to think."

What a thoughtful thug. "How long are you going to keep me here?"

"Are you going to help me?"

"I'm thinking about it."

He pointed to a chair in the corner. "Good. When you decide, I'll be over there." He sat, folded his arms across his chest, and closed his eyes.

I weighed my options. If I told him no, he would probably torture my family until I agreed. That made the other choice—helping him find Finn so he could kill him and ride off into the sunset—seem like a no-brainer.

"I've decided to help you," I said.

Vincent opened his eyes and smiled. "Good choice."

I chose a hard place instead of a rock.

He pulled out his phone and started tapping, then set the phone on the desk. He rested his elbows on his knees and leaned forward. "How is this going to work?"

"First, you're going to turn off your phone." I paused. "Nice try, but whatever we say in this room stays in this room."

He hesitated, then tapped his phone a few times.

"And next, you're going to untie me."

More hesitation.

If he wanted my help, he would do it. I waited. He pulled out a knife and cut the ties.

I rubbed my wrists. "Let me see your phone."

He handed it to me. I verified it was off, then handed it back to him.

"I'll call you as soon as I find out where Rafferty is," I said.

"How do I know you'll do that?"

"I want to see my family again. I assume that's the deal."

He nodded his enormous head.

"I want him dead as much as you do... maybe more. I'll make the call, then try to stall the sheriff to buy you some time, but you're going to have to act fast. Once we determine his location, the sheriff is going to want to pick him up ASAP. I'll hold up my end of the deal. What you do with the information and when you do it, is on you."

"Don't worry about me. You just get me the information."

"And then I never see you again, right?"

"That's right."

"When do I see Jenn and Alex again?"

"After you hold up your end of the deal, and I'm gone, I'll send you instructions where to find them."

"What if the sheriff comes looking for you?"

"This isn't my first rodeo," he said. "No one will know Vincent the big ugly guy was even there, let alone where to find him." He grinned and shook his head. "No, sir. He'll be long gone. And it wouldn't be the first time I've had to disappear. I'm getting real good at it."

"When we find him, how do I get in touch with you?"

He pulled a small burner phone from his pocket and tossed it to me. "Use this. The number is programmed in."

Lawman Luke would be so proud.

Vincent dropped me off at my truck and disappeared into the night. After strapping on my gun and checking my phone, I dropped Jenn's phone into an evidence bag that I had in the truck. If the lab could pull a print off her phone, I might be able to put a last name to that big ugly face.

***

I arrived home just before midnight. The black sky opened up and released a deluge of rain. I sat in my truck and waited, stuck between a rock and a hard place again. I reckoned sometimes you did what you needed to do to get by. Probably what every murderer on death row said at one time or another.

The rain slowed, and I made a run for the house. Inside, I paced around the living room in my wet clothes. Sleep would not come easy tonight without a cup of rain dance tea. I put the kettle on and left the room, fearing it would never boil if I stood by and watched.

It bothered me that what Vincent wanted me to do didn't bother me. Part of me wanted him to succeed. Finn would be out of our lives, and I wouldn't need to get my hands dirty. I would make one phone call. That's not illegal, right?

To be honest, it bothered me a little, but my priority was to get Jenn and Alex back safely. I couldn't let anything, including my conscience, get in the way. Job one was to find Finn as quickly as possible.

The kettle squealed in the kitchen, and I made my tea. Some might say a six-pack would be the medicine of choice, but I knew better. I felt the tea's calming effects after the first few sips.

I needed something else. Something I hadn't been able to do for the better part of my life. I needed to talk to Mama. I dialed her number.

"Hey, Mama."

"Dillon? It's late. Is everything all right?"

"I just need to talk."

"What's the matter?"

"Do you think the end always justifies the means?"

"Sometimes, I guess it does. Give me an example."

"Family. How far would you go to protect your family?"

She hesitated. "I think it's ironic that you would ask such a question of me."

"That was then, Mama. I'm talking about now."

"I would do almost anything."

"What if that anything might be considered illegal?"

"You're scaring me, Dillon. Are Jenn and Alex okay?"

"I'm going to have to do something I shouldn't to protect them."

"You're not going to tell me what that is, are you?"

"I can't."

"You need to follow your heart. I just hope it's something you can live with."

"In the end, that decision is mine, I reckon. I just needed to talk to someone."

"You know someone in Heaven who might help."

"Who? Daddy?"

"He wasn't the first one to come to mind, but I guess he might be able to help if he's sober." She paused. "I was thinking of your brother."

"I talk to Luke sometimes."

"That's nice. He used to look up to you. He would be so proud of you wearing that badge."

I couldn't bring myself to tell her I might lose it. "I reckon you're right."

"Do you remember that Halloween when he dressed up as the sheriff? We couldn't get him out that costume for a week." She paused. "What did we used to call him?"

"Lawman Luke."

A long silence settled in, and I thought I heard her cry. "Luke is gonna be fine, Mama. He's probably keeping the peace in Heaven as we speak."

"I know. You always have our prayers. I believe you're going to get through this."

"Maybe we can all get together this summer."

"That would be nice. In the meantime, if you ever need us, you know you can just call, and we'll be there."

"Thanks Mama. You tell Mort I said hey."

"You do the same to Jenn and Alex. I love you, son." Her voice was brittle. "Always have and always will."

I believed her, and it made me smile. "Love you, too, Mama."

In the morning, I would go into the office and send Finn's picture to all the motel owners in a twenty-five-mile radius, asking them to call the sheriff's office if they'd seen him. I needed to control the situation, so I wouldn't send an APB to other area law enforcement agencies.

It had been a long, trying day, and there was nothing more I could do from home. I didn't want to sleep alone in that big bed, so I turned on the TV and reclined in the La-Z-Boy. Not much to watch at one o'clock in the morning, unless you need laser hair removal or a weight-loss miracle. The distraction wasn't enough to keep me from wondering where Jenn and Alex were and how they were being treated. Vincent said they were safe. They wouldn't be safe until they were back home with me.

Chapter Twenty-One

I awoke early and drove into the office to send Finn's picture out from the official department email address. I wrote the message, attached the photo, and hit send. The coffee pot belched out the end of its cycle, and I poured myself a cup.

"I thought I told you to take the weekend off," Ziggy said as he walked through the bullpen to his office.

"What can I say..." I smiled. "I love my job."

"What's so important that you had to come in on a Sunday?"

"I could ask you the same thing."

He shook his head. "I don't want to be here, but Ferg is sick. What's your excuse?"

"Jenn's not home, and I didn't feel like hanging around the house." *Oops!*

He poured himself a cup of coffee. "Where'd she go?"

"Uh... I don't know." *That part was true.* "She took Alex shopping someplace." *Time to change the subject.* "I sent Finn's picture to all the local motels, hoping somebody has seen him recently."

"Good idea. You should send out an APB, as well." He leaned against one of the desks. "Call me if you get a hit. I don't want you going in without backup."

I raised an eyebrow. "You can say it."

"Alright. Given your history with the man, I think I should be there."

"Roger that."

Ziggy lingered for a moment, no doubt to let his words sink in, before disappearing into his office.

I followed him in. "One more thing. I matched the most-called number on Kayla's phone to Finn."

"Good work. That should be enough to get a warrant."

I needed to leave before I put my foot in my mouth again. I had no way to explain where Jenn was without exposing my plan. That wouldn't be helping anyone. Avoiding everyone I knew seemed like the best course of action, at least for the rest of the day. The department email account could only be accessed from the office, so I planned to monitor the radio and slip back in if Ziggy went out on a call.

I drove down Route 67 toward Redfield, wondering what to do with myself for the rest of the day. Ziggy's shift ended at five. If I showed up again before he left, he'd have more questions, including why I didn't send out the APB.

Who was Vincent, and where had he taken Jenn and Alex? The only lead I had was a possible fingerprint on Jenn's phone. It sat inside an evidence bag in the console. I struggled with how I might get any prints lifted and matched. Hattie had hooked me up with a crime lab in Denver last year, but I was reluctant to ask her for help. I would have considered it if Ziggy wasn't her son.

Coop appeared to be my only option. I hesitated to involve him in my troubles once again after he'd taken a bullet for me the first time, but I was out of options. The fact that he lived in Texas offered a level of safety that I could live with.

I called Coop when I got back to the ranch.

"What have you gotten yourself into this time?"

"What's the matter? Can't I call my old friend once in a while just to catch up?"

A moment of silence passed. "Sorry. It's just that—"

"I need your help."

"There's the Dillon I remember."

"I need to pull some fingerprints from a cell phone."

"In case you forgot, I don't have a crime lab in my garage."

"What about Jimmy?"

Jimmy Arroyo had been the third of our *Three Amigos* in high school. We'd done everything together, then gone our separate ways. Jimmy had been the brains of our trio, a real computer nerd, so it was no surprise that he'd landed a job as Security Systems Product Manager with a big tech firm in Arlington. He'd helped me out of a jam back in Texas with his connections and some high-tech surveillance equipment.

"Why don't you let the sheriff take care of it?"

"I need to use some discretion on this one."

"Jimmy can probably help you out, but only if you tell me what's going on."

"I'd rather not."

"Seriously? After I took a bullet for you?"

I knew I'd never hear the end of that one. I hesitated. "For your ears only."

"Of course."

"Jenn and Alex have been kidnapped by this big, ugly dude."

"What?! You're kidding. Tell me you're kidding."

"I wish I was."

"Why Jenn and Alex?"

"To get to me."

"Jeezus, Bish. This is serious. You need to get the sheriff involved, maybe even the state police."

"I can't do that. He's holding her until I do something that might be considered... obstructing justice, or conspiracy to commit murder, or both, and I'm not in a position to call his bluff."

"Do you need me to come out there?"

"Thanks, but no. I'm sending you her phone because he might have left a print on it. I need you to help me put a name to the prints."

"Okay. FedEx me the phone and I'll drive it up to Arlington. I'll call Jimmy as soon as we get off the phone to set it up."

"I have a first name that may or may not be real. He called himself Vincent."

"Got it. I'll call you tomorrow with an update."

"Thanks, Coop. I owe you."

"Yeah, you do."

I arranged for same-day service online, and they picked up the package an hour later. The rest of the afternoon felt like a week. I drove into the office around five-thirty, after I heard Ziggy sign off for the day. He would be on call, but not at the station.

No replies from any of the motel owners. I let out a breath. My stomach rumbled to let me know I needed to eat something. Where did Finn eat? I made a list of area restaurants, particularly those that did takeout, and sent a similar email with Finn's picture. This significantly increased my chances of getting a hit. The man had to eat.

I sat around clicking the *check email* button. If a response came in now, I could mark it as unread, call Vincent, and pretend I was reading it for the first time in the morning. He'd have plenty of time to take care of business, and I could notify Ziggy as soon as I read it again in the morning—no stalling required.

I sat at my desk for the next two hours, clicking that mouse every five minutes. *Nothing.* My stomach complained so violently, I finally left the office for a burger and a beer at the Wet Whistle.

CHAPTER TWENTY-TWO

I noticed something odd as soon as I walked through the front door. Buck and the Whitehawk brothers sat together in a corner booth. They stopped talking when they noticed me. Buck looked as nervous as a hooker in church when I walked up to their table.

"What's wrong with this picture?" I smiled.

I got a *hey,* a couple of grunts, and the feeling that they didn't want me around.

"So, what brings you boys out tonight?"

They looked at each other for a moment before Jacob spoke. "Buck, here's got a new girlfriend."

"Really, Buck? Anybody I know?"

Buck didn't look well and avoided my eyes.

"She owns a hardware store," Jeremiah said, "and he was lookin' for a screw."

I waited for Buck to say something, but all I got was a *you-better-keep-your-trap-shut* glare.

"I heard he got his tool sharpened," Jacob said, and nudged his brother.

Buck waved a dismissing hand. "Aww, don't listen to these fools."

An uncomfortable silence descended on the table.

"Okay, then, I'm gonna grab something to eat at the bar."

Three bobbleheads nodded their approval.

I pulled up a stool at the long, wooden bar and ordered a Coors. "Kitchen still open?"

The bartender nodded. "I'll send a waitress your way."

I glanced back at the corner table. The boys had resumed their discussion.

A waitress emerged from the kitchen wearing an apron with *Don't Make Me Poison Your Food* printed across the front. "What can I get you, cowboy?"

"Bacon burger, fries..." I held up my bottle. "And another one of these."

She wrote it down and disappeared into the kitchen.

The Wet Whistle wasn't known for its speedy food service, but it was a slow night. She slid my plate across the bar ten minutes later, and I inhaled the food. I realized I hadn't eaten all day and ordered another.

While I waited for the second round, I snuck a sideways glance in Buck's direction. We'd gotten off to a rough start when I moved here, but we eventually became trusted friends. I hesitated to confide in anyone about my present predicament, even Buck. Given his love of Jenn and the ranch, his eagerness to help might turn him into a loose cannon. I needed to play this one close to the vest.

I checked on Buck's table when I finished round two. The boys sat alone, talking to each other. I picked up what was left of my beer and walked over to their table.

"Where's Buck?"

They answered simultaneously with different answers. Jacob said he was in the bathroom, and Jeremiah claimed he went home.

I smiled. "I think you boys might have had a little too much to drink." I paused. "Which is it?"

They answered in unison again but switched their answers. I waited.

"He went to the bathroom, then he went home," Jacob said.

"He said real men don't get sick," Jeremiah added. "He didn't want you to see him and think he was a pussy."

Heckle and Jeckle glanced at each other and stifled a laugh.

My crack security team. I shook my head. "That's okay. I wanted to talk to you two."

I called the waitress over and ordered a round of drinks.

"How would you go about finding someone you know nothing about?" I asked when she left.

"Why do you need to find someone if you don't know them?"

Jacob elbowed his brother. "Do you have a name?"

"I have a first name and a picture."

"Show me the picture."

I pulled Vincent's picture from my pocket and handed it to him.

Jeremiah leaned in to get a look. "Scary dude."

Not helping.

Jacob nodded and handed it back. "Why do you want to find him?"

"Let's just say he has something of mine, and I want it back."

Our drinks came, and I paid the waitress.

I lifted an eyebrow. "Isn't one of you supposed to be watching the ranch?"

"Buck gave us the night off."

"The new guys are covering." Jacob said.

"We need a night off once in a while, you know?" Jeremiah took a swig from his bottle before the bobbleheads started again.

We talked for a half hour about the ranch, the new hires, the casino, and life in general. I told them I had to work in the morning and bought them another round before I said my goodbyes.

"Let me know if you want us to find that scary dude for you," Jacob called as I headed for the door.

"Roger that."

***

The four beers I'd had the night before allowed me to skip the tea and save it in case things with Vincent went sideways. I checked email as soon as I arrived at work. No one had replied to my inquiries about Finn.

Ziggy responded to an early call, leaving me to hold down the fort with Ruby, the dispatcher. I poured another cup of coffee and paced around the office. It might be days before someone responded to my emails. If I could just talk to Jenn, maybe I could relax a little. I pulled the burner phone from my pocket and hit speed dial.

"Did you find him?"

"Not yet. Just testing the comm channel for when I do." I paused. "Let me speak to Jenn."

"She's not here. Don't worry, they're both safe."

Seriously? Don't worry? "How do I know that?"

"You just worry about finding Rafferty."

The line went dead. *That didn't help.* I couldn't sit, so I got up and walked out front. I passed Ruby's empty desk and found her outside with a cigarette between her fingers.

I nodded politely. "Ma'am."

"You look like you could use a smoke," she said.

Despite my sour mood, I mustered a half smile. "A drink would be more like it."

"Amen." She nodded. "But all I got are cigarettes."

I studied her. She looked to be about Mama's age, with red hair, a few extra pounds, and a little too much makeup. "Those things'll kill you."

She took a long drag and turned her head away to exhale. The cloud drifted and quickly dispersed. "I only smoke at work," she replied as she turned back toward me.

"My girlfriend doesn't like it when I light up at home," I said.

"Oh, Harold don't mind all that much. It's them damn oxygen tanks he has to cart around."

"I'm sorry…"

"Don't be." She waved a dismissing hand. "He smoked two packs a day for thirty-five years. He had it coming."

I wasn't sure what to say.

"You're not from around here. Where do you hail from?"

"Born and raised in Texas."

"That explains it."

"Explains what?"

"Yes, ma'am. No, ma'am. That southern charm."

"Why, thank you, but I don't know how charming I am."

"You're right. You don't. My boys talk to me like truck drivers."

"I'm sorry to hear that." She should have heard how I talked to Mama when she showed up after going AWOL for sixteen years.

"If you ever need anything, you can ask Aunt Ruby." She smiled at me like she was talking to her favorite nephew.

"Yes, ma'am."

She flashed a big smile before crushing out what was left of her cigarette. "See? Charming."

Talking to Aunt Ruby had taken the edge off, but had only used up ten minutes. I honestly didn't know how I would make it through the rest of the day.

A man showed up complaining about vandals who'd defaced the side of his building. He operated the truck stop located down the road a half mile. Ruby ushered him into the bullpen. I welcomed the distraction and took his statement. He brought in video from his security camera, which I logged and told him we'd review it and get back to him.

I plugged the thumb drive into my computer after he left. My phone rang as I reviewed the first file.

The owner of the Golden Bear Inn near Cripple Creek told me he'd received my email and called to let me know that the man in the photo had rented a room at his motel.

"Are you sure it's him?"

"One hundred percent. He stopped in the office last night to pay for another day."

"Where is he now?"

"His car's in the lot, so I'm guessing he's in his room. Number 117."

"Does he drive a green Toyota?"

"That's the one."

"I'll be there shortly. Call me if he leaves."

"Will do."

I hit speed dial on the burner.

"This better not be another test."

"I found him," I said. "He's at the Golden Bear Inn on 67, about a mile north of Cripple Creek. Room 117. I'll wait a half hour before I call the sheriff."

"That'll work."

"Now tell me where Jenn and Alex are."

The line went dead.

I let a couple of colorful expletives fly, which brought Ruby to the doorway.

"Is everything alright?"

I apologized and assured her everything was okay. I checked the time on my phone. Twenty-eight more minutes. I told myself that Big Ugly Vincent hadn't just double-crossed me. He wouldn't release Jenn and Alex until the job was done, and he was on his way out of the county. That made sense. That's what I would do.

The only thing that would get me through the next... twenty-six minutes, would be knowing that Finn Rafferty would soon be out of our lives for good.

CHAPTER TWENTY-THREE

P recisely thirty minutes after the call came in, I notified Ziggy. I gave him the location and told him I would meet him there."

"You stay put. Bill and I will check it out."

"But I want to be there when—"

"Bill's here with me. We're ten minutes away. We've got this."

Sorry, Zig, but I gotta be there. "Roger that."

I asked Aunt Ruby to cover for me.

"Be careful," she called after me as I left the station in a hurry.

Ziggy had a fifteen-minute head start. I didn't want to miss the party, so I flipped on the lights and siren.

The door to Room 117 was open when I pulled into the parking lot. Two sheriff's vehicles and the coroner's van were parked just outside a perimeter marked by yellow police tape. It appeared that Vincent had already been there.

I ducked under the yellow tape.

Ziggy stepped in front of me. "What are you doing here?"

"Gimme a break, Zig. This is personal."

"Exactly why I told you to stay at the station." Ziggy's eyes told me we were going to have some words later.

I pretended not to notice. "What do we have here?"

"It's him. He's dead."

I let out the breath I'd been holding for the last three months. "What happened?"

"It looks like a suicide."

Well played, Vincent.

The coroner examined the body as we spoke.

"Nothing official yet?"

"I imagine we'll have to wait for the autopsy."

I leaned in to get a better look.

Ziggy grabbed my arm and pulled me back. "I need to get back to work, and you need—"

"Hey, Sheriff." Bill interrupted. "Over here."

Ziggy turned to Bill, then back to me. "Don't touch anything." He turned his attention to Bill.

I wandered over toward the bed where Finn's body sat propped against the headboard. The top of his head had been blown off, painting the wall behind the bed with blood and brain tissue. As bad as it looked, I couldn't bring myself to feel anything but relief.

The shot had come from under his chin, a popular suicide angle. The gun lay across his open hand at his side. My stomach tied itself in a knot when I recognized the Glock 9mm with the silencer on the end. I'd held that gun less than two weeks ago. My prints were probably still on it.

The CSU photographer nudged me out of the way, and I stumbled backward on rubber legs.

Bill showed Ziggy what looked like a bullet hole near the inside of the door frame. The CSU tech joined them. Finn might have gotten a shot off when Vincent entered the room. If they found that it came from Finn's gun, it would be inconsistent with a suicide.

People seemed to move in slow motion, everyone busy with their assigned tasks. I felt like a ghost as I stood and watched.

Ziggy gave me the stink eye, and I left the room, thankful for the fresh air. The burner phone hadn't rung yet. What was Vincent waiting for? I'd tipped him off as promised. Finn was dead. So where were Jenn and Alex?

I sat in the Bronco, staring at the phone, willing it to ring. After ten minutes, I pushed speed dial. No answer. I tried to convince myself to be patient. Vincent had just killed a man. He had to cover his tracks and lay low. He would call soon. After that, I never wanted to see his ugly face again.

Maybe Vincent didn't pull the trigger. Maybe he had Fishlips do it for him. As long as Finn was headed for the morgue, I didn't care who put him there.

Unfortunately, Ziggy cared.

He knocked on my window. "Why are you still here?"

"I thought I'd stick around in case you need help."

"I don't. Nothing else to see. CSU will be here for a while, and they don't need anyone getting in the way."

"Looks open and shut. Suicide, right?"

"Looks that way, but I'm not so sure."

I avoided his eyes. "What do you mean?"

"Ruby called. I need you to go take a statement from John Stevens and help him round up his horses. Someone busted up part of his fence and let them out."

Sounded like a good excuse to get rid of me. "Sure."

"Get the information from Ruby on your way."

"Roger that."

I stepped on the accelerator a little too hard and burned rubber on the way out of the parking lot. *I'm sure I'll hear about that later.*

My nerves felt like a frayed wire about to snap. Finn was dead. That was good news, but I had a feeling Ziggy knew it was murder and would like me for the crime when they found my prints on the murder weapon. I certainly had motive, but if everyone who wanted to kill someone acted on it, there'd be nobody left.

I had bigger problems, like getting Jenn and Alex back. I felt double-crossed and helpless to do anything about it, but waiting was not something I did well. I called Coop, hoping for some good news. He'd received Jenn's phone last night and driven it up to Arlington. Jimmy said he knew someone who could get him an answer within twenty-four hours. He would call me directly as soon as he had the results.

John Stevens owned approximately one hundred twenty acres northeast of Jenn's land in the Riverdale target zone. I pulled into his drive and watched two men chase a bunch of horses around a field. I joined them a few minutes later, and we spent the next two hours rounding up twenty-three horses and mending the broken fence.

"Did Buck tell you about the meeting here tonight?" John asked when we finished.

"No. I'm not sure that's such a good idea after what happened the last time."

He leaned in closer. "That's why we're doing it." He hesitated. "I probably shouldn't be telling you this, but I need your help."

"I'm not sure I follow you."

"It's a trap. Hopefully, the son of a bitch that torched Hank's barn will be back to try to do the same to mine. I'm asking you to be here when he does."

"What if he doesn't show?"

"He'll show." He lowered his voice. "I think there's a mole in the group. All the same folks will be there."

"I don't think you have a mole."

"Why do you say that?"

"I heard someone posing as a BLM agent has been talking to the ranchers, but he's dead. So, maybe your problem is solved."

"Which one?" he asked with a wary expression.

I shook my head. "I'm not at liberty to say."

"I mean, which agent?"

"There's more than one?" I assumed Finn worked alone.

"Two that I know of."

I scratched the space above my lip. "Sounds like you still have a problem."

"Can you help us?"

"You want me to arrest him?"

"I don't care if you blow his damn head off."

Given my present state of mind, I couldn't rule out the latter. "I can arrest him and charge him with trespassing and arson. Maybe we can get him to flip on whoever he's working for."

"I sure would appreciate it."

Normally, I'd run something like this by Ziggy, but he'd just told me he didn't need me around. That worked both ways. "Sure. When do you want me here?"

"The meeting starts at eight. You're welcome to attend, or you can get here at ten when we break up."

"I'll be here. Not sure when."

My mind spun faster than my tires on the way back to the station. I felt pulled in too many directions at once. Something would have to give, and I was afraid it might be my sanity. I still hadn't heard from Vincent, Ziggy had me at the top of the suspect list for Finn's death, and I'd just agreed to an unsanctioned stakeout to catch an arsonist who's terrorizing ranches in Riverdale's target area. Jenn's ranch was the biggest fish in that sea.

At the station, I stood in Ziggy's doorway.

"How did it go at the motel?"

He leaned back in his chair. "It's looking less like a suicide, but I haven't ruled that out yet."

I nodded as casually as I could, not sure what I should say.

"I know how much trouble he caused you," Ziggy said after an uncomfortable silence.

He didn't know the half of it.

"If I were you, I'd be dancing a happy dance." He paused and held my gaze. "Unless there's something you're not telling me."

"Nothing I can think of." I shifted my weight to the other foot and hooked a thumb toward my desk. "I should probably get back to work." I turned.

"Dillon, wait."

I stopped and turned around slowly.

"What happened at John Stevens' place?"

I blew out a breath. "Looks like someone let his horses out. Took three of us a couple of hours to round 'em up and fix the fence."

"Any leads?"

"Nothing. Sounds to me like more Riverdale threats."

When I returned to my desk, I watched more security video from the truck stop. It made me wonder if Jenn and Alex were still in Colorado, or if Vincent had left town with them. I lost count of how many times I glanced at the clock on the wall. The burner phone was burning a hole in my pocket.

I hurried past Ruby, stepped outside, and hit speed dial.

"What do you want?" Vincent asked.

"I want my family back. Tell me where they are."

"Rafferty was dead when I got there."

I closed my eyes and shook my head. "What are you talking about?"

"Sheriff passed me on the way out. Were you trying to set me up?"

"Absolutely not." I tried to wrap my head around what he'd just said. "Are you telling me you didn't kill him?"

"I told you, he was dead when I got there. Looked like he offed himself."

I didn't believe him, but I went along with it to avoid being considered a loose end that he needed to tighten up. Eventually, I might convince myself that I wasn't a co-conspirator.

"So, where does that leave us?" I didn't wait for an answer. "I held up my end of the deal. Now you need to let my family go."

A few seconds of silence passed. "I can't do that."

CHAPTER TWENTY-FOUR

M y heart sank below my stomach. "Why not?"

"I'm still out twenty grand."

"That's not my problem. You said if he couldn't pay, you'd kill him. He couldn't pay, he's dead, you got what you wanted."

"I want my twenty grand."

I didn't like where this was headed. He held all the cards. I didn't know who he was, or where he had Jenn.

"I'm not paying you twenty-thousand dollars."

"You're right. It's twenty-five when you include interest."

"That's insane."

"I would think your family was worth at least that." He paused, letting his words sink in. "You offered to pay Rafferty to go away. The only thing that's changed is the name."

Outsmarted by a Sasquatch. "You son of a bitch."

The line went dead.

My temperature rose fifteen degrees, and I stopped just short of throwing the phone against the side of the building. I took a deep breath and returned to my desk to resume watching the truck stop security video.

I finished the first drive and plugged in the second. More of the same brick wall. I sat back in my chair, finding it difficult to concentrate on the screen with Vincent still holding Jenn and Alex. The money Finn owed was not part of our deal. I considered bringing Ziggy in but decided to wait until I had the results back from Jimmy.

Movement on the screen pulled me away from my thoughts. Some numbnuts wearing a hoodie and his pants halfway down his backside entered the frame. He looked around, all nervous and jerky, then pulled out a can of spray paint and went to work.

"Gotcha!"

I zoomed in, printed a copy, and gave it to Ruby to distribute.

An uneventful afternoon followed, and I reminded Ziggy that I wouldn't be working the next day. I'd worked nearly every day for the past week and needed to get back to our agreed upon every-other-day schedule. The Vincent issue needed more of my attention.

On the way home, I called John Stevens, but Coop called in before we finished. I told John I'd be there by ten, then switched calls.

"Did you get anything?"

"Hello, Coop. Hello, Dillon," Coop said with a healthy dose of sarcasm.

"Sorry. I'm a little on edge."

"Understandable." He paused. "Jimmy got a full print off the phone and matched it to a Vincent Courtemanche from De-troit."

"Detroit? What's he doing out here?"

"He lives in Wyoming now. Works security at a casino out there. Got a rap sheet two pages long."

"I'm not surprised. Let me guess... the casino is owned by Riverdale Gaming."

"Yeah. How'd you know?"

"Lucky guess."

I told him about Vincent's latest demand. It would take time to get the money together, and I had no reason to trust that Vincent would let them go if I did. Coop suggested I don't wait too long before getting someone like Brickman involved.

Hattie had recommended Dave Brickman, a lieutenant with the Colorado State Police, last year when we got in a jam over Uncle Roy's death. He'd been partners with her husband on the force and had considerable pull within the department.

I found myself between a rock and a hard place again. Brickman might be able to help, but I couldn't risk a state police investigation. Not yet.

I thanked Coop and told him I'd be in touch.

When I arrived home, I slipped my key into the lock. My chest tightened and made it difficult to breathe. I hesitated, dreading the silence that awaited me inside. I'd spent many years in self-imposed exile where silence was a trusted friend, but Jenn and Alex had changed all that, and I couldn't go back. I told myself familiar voices would return to echo off these walls, but I didn't like how hard I had to work to convince myself.

I walked back down the steps and headed toward the cabins. Jacob answered the door when I knocked.

"I need your help," I said.

Jeremiah appeared at his side. "Is this about that scary dude?"

"His name is Vincent Courtemanche, and I need you to find him."

"What did he do?"

I hesitated as I debated how much to tell them. The gravity of the situation necessitated they know what they were dealing with. "He's holding Jenn and Alex for ransom."

Their jaws dropped in unison.

"Nobody got through that gate," Jacob assured me.

"Relax. I'm not here to scold you. They were abducted on the way home from dinner."

They nodded, and their expressions softened.

"I need to find him before he hurts them."

"Did you call the police?" Jeremiah asked.

Jacob turned to his brother. "He *is* the police."

"I need to take care of this myself." I paused. "It's complicated."

"Are you going to pay the ransom?"

"I'm hoping you can find him, and I can take him out before it gets to that."

"What do you want us to do when we find him?"

"Nothing. I don't want to give him any reason to hurt my family. I need you to contact me and sit tight."

"We can do that," Jacob said.

I told them about the construction trailer near Cripple Creek where I had been held. I remembered hearing a train pass nearby. It wasn't much to go on, but I figured it would be a good place to start.

"I'll pay you a thousand dollars," I said.

They looked at each other. Jeremiah spoke. "Each?"

"Depends on how quickly you find them."

They nodded in unison.

I returned to my truck and thought about killing some time at the Wet Whistle before driving over to the Stevens place, but I didn't want to show up for the stakeout with alcohol on my breath.

Buck knocked on my window.

"Haven't seen Jenn and the boy around. Are they alright?"

I saw no reason not to let Buck in on what happened. "Have you eaten yet?"

He shook his head.

"Hop in. I'll buy you dinner."

He hesitated. "Thanks, but—"

"Get in. I've got something to tell you."

Buck climbed in and we headed for the Bluebird.

"Did you hear Finn's dead?" I asked.

"Good riddance."

"I think I know who killed him."

He stared out the window. "I heard it was a suicide."

"I wish."

"Did you arrest whoever did it?"

"No. He's got Jenn and Alex."

Buck's head turned so fast in my direction, I thought it might snap off his neck and land on the seat between us. "What!?"

"It's a long story. I'll tell you over dinner."

After a waitress seated us and took our order, I said, "I haven't told Ziggy any of this, so it's just between you and me."

Buck nodded as he gnawed on a breadstick like it owed him money.

"I took Jenn and Alex here the night it happened. A man named Vincent Courtemanche abducted us on the way home."

"All of you?"

"Yes. He had an accomplice, and they split us up. I haven't seen Jenn since."

"How'd you get away?"

"He was looking for information on Finn, and he let me go to find it. He said if I told him where Finn was hiding, he would release Jenn and Alex."

"Did you tell him?"

I shook my head. "That's not important. Finn owed him a lot of money, which he can no longer pay, so now he wants it from me."

Buck frowned. "What are you going to do?"

"I need to find him, so I asked Jacob and Jeremiah to help."

"You don't want to get the sheriff involved?"

"No. If I can't find him soon, I reckon I'll pay him and hope for the best."

"I don't like it. You all have seen his face. That usually means…" He drew a finger sideways across his throat.

Not helping.

Buck's eyes narrowed. "If there's anything I can do…"

"I'll let you know." I checked the time on my phone. "Want a ride to the meeting tonight?"

"Sure. My truck's in the shop."

The waitress arrived with the check, and I gave her a credit card.

"What are you doing after the meeting?"

Buck offered a tentative smile. "I don't know, but I reckon you're fixin' to tell me."

When we reached the Stevens place, I parked the Bronco out of sight. Buck went inside while I walked around the grounds, gathering intel before I joined him.

The mixture of fear and vigilante justice that hung in the stale air met me at the door. I took a seat in the back and listened to their impassioned speeches before they opened the floor for discussion.

The meeting broke up just before ten, but John, Buck and a couple of others stayed behind. John introduced me to the group, and we discussed plans for the rest of the evening. I questioned whether the person who burned down Hank's barn would attempt another one so soon. Would he use the same M.O. again, setting the fire after another meeting? But I didn't want to read about it in the paper tomorrow, knowing that I might have had a chance to stop it.

John gave us each a thermos filled with coffee and a small two-way radio, and we took up positions on different sides of the barn. I hoped I'd be the one to apprehend the perp, in case he was armed. The others knew what they'd signed up for, but I didn't want to see anyone get hurt on my watch.

Time passed slowly, and I struggled to keep my mind on the task at hand. Inevitably, it circled back to Jenn's situation as I ran through every possible scenario.

At eleven forty, I stood to stretch my legs and detected movement through the brush. I flipped my night vision goggles down and crept toward the barn. I reached the barn and found no one outside, but the door had been left open a few inches.

Gasoline burned the back of my throat when I stepped inside, and I buried my nose in the crook of my arm. I fought the urge to draw my sidearm for fear that one shot might blow the roof off the barn. I had the advantage of being able to see him in the blackness and moved closer.

I flipped up my goggles and turned on my flashlight. "Need a match?"

CHAPTER TWENTY-FIVE

The intruder dropped the gasoline can and ran past me out the door. I chased him along the side of the barn.

"He's coming your way, Buck," I said into the radio.

He turned the corner of the barn and went down like he'd hit a brick wall. Or more precisely, a Buck wall. Buck pinned him with a move that would have made Hulk Hogan proud.

I rolled the perp over, cuffed him, and dragged him to his feet.

Buck stood and brushed himself off, smiling like I was Starsky and he was Hutch.

I gave him a smile and an *attaboy* nod.

The perp looked as scared as a sinner in a cyclone when I sat him down in the dirt against the wall. The others arrived, and we commenced with a barrage of questions, but he refused to answer any of them. I thought my uniform might intimidate him into coming clean. It didn't.

I turned to Buck. "Get me his can of gasoline from inside."

When he left, I removed my hat and handed it to John. He held it upside down, and I dropped my badge inside.

Buck returned and handed me the gas can.

The perp's expression changed from defiance to fear. "What are you going to do with that?"

"Let's try this again." I removed the cap and splashed some on his shirt. "We'll start with your name."

He looked down at his shirt, then up at me. Fear became terror.

I splashed some more down the front of his pants. His body bounced a few inches off the ground, and he kicked his legs until he fell onto his side. I grabbed him by the collar and straightened him up.

"You're not going anywhere," I said. "Anybody got a lighter?"

John stepped in front of me. "Maybe that's enough."

"Do you want to know who tried to burn down your barn, or don't you?"

He shrunk a little and handed me his lighter. I flipped it open and flicked it a couple of times until a flame appeared.

"What did you say your name was?"

"Marty."

"Marty what?"

"Rogers."

"Now we're getting somewhere."

"Can you close that thing?"

I snapped my wrist, and the lighter closed with a click. "I'll hang on to this in case I need it again."

"You won't," he said. "But you gotta understand. They're gonna kill me like they did the other guy."

"What other guy?"

"The one they found in the motel room."

"Today?" When I recovered from the initial shock, I opened the lighter. "What do you know about that?"

"I know I'm next."

I pulled Finn's picture from my pocket and held it in front of his face. "You know him?"

He nodded.

I closed the lighter and pulled him up by one arm. "We're going for a ride."

"Where?"

"County jail."

He looked relieved.

"What's going to happen to him?" John asked.

"Depends on whether you want to press charges. In the meantime, I can hold him overnight and try to find out who put him up to this."

"Thanks." He let out a breath.

"You got any clean clothes for him to change into?" I didn't want Marty to stink up my vehicle or the sheriff's station or make me have to explain to Ziggy why his clothes were soaked in gasoline.

John nodded.

"You got anyplace I could hose him down first?"

John met us at the stables with some fresh clothes, a towel, and a bar of soap. He led us to where he hosed down the horses. I tossed Marty the soap and towel and told him to have at it.

John agreed to give Buck a ride home while I drove Marty back to the station. When we got there, I locked him in the holding cell and put on a pot of coffee.

I pulled a chair up to the cell and studied him through the bars. He was sweating like a hooker in church.

"What's going to happen to me?" he asked.

"I caught you red-handed, Marty." I shook my head. "I'm not gonna lie, you're looking at some serious jail time."

He wrung his hands. "They made me do it. I didn't have a choice."

"Here's what we're gonna do. I'll get us some coffee, then you're gonna tell me everything. If the information helps us with this case, I'll put in a good word and see if maybe the judge will reduce your sentence for cooperating."

"I'm scared."

"We'll do everything we can to protect you."

He nodded his head. I left him staring at the floor while I headed for the coffee pot.

I returned with two cups and handed one through the bars. Marty took it with a shaking hand.

"Where do you live?"

"Cheyenne, Wyoming."

"What are you doing starting fires in Colorado?"

He stared into his cup. "It's a long story."

"You're not going anywhere, and we've got plenty of coffee."

"I'm embarrassed to say."

"Well, suck it up, buttercup. Let's start from the beginning."

He took a gulp of coffee, then ran the back of his hand across his lips. "I got played."

"How so?"

"I was at the casino, winning for a change, when this pretty young thing sat down next to me. She got all caught up in it and started cheering me on. The more I won, the more handsy she got. I gotta tell ya, it felt pretty good. Then she started pushing me to make bigger bets."

He paused, and I waited.

"Pretty soon, I lost it all." He shook his head. "How could I have been so stupid?"

"Anybody might have done the same in that situation."

He took in a long breath and let it out slowly. "It gets worse."

I waited.

"She told me where I could get a quick loan right there at the casino. Said I still had some of that hot streak left and could win it all back and then some. She put her hand on my privates and said we could stop at her room on the way back."

"Okay, that was a little stupid." I shook my head. "Let me guess. You went up there, took off your pants, and some big dude comes in and steals your money."

"Stole my pants, too."

All attempts to hide my amusement failed.

"It's not funny."

"Sorry. Please continue."

"So, now I owe them five grand with no way to pay it off. I'm between jobs and a month behind on my rent."

And you're spending time at the casino. I held up Vincent's picture. "Is this the guy who robbed you?"

"No, it was the other one."

"What other one?"

"The bald one with the big lips."

Fishlips. "Does he have a name?"

"Carlo. I don't know his last name."

"But you've seen the guy in the picture?"

He nodded. "I think they both worked security at the casino."

"How did you know Finn?"

"Same thing happened to him."

"He told you that?"

"Yep. I met him shortly after I got here. They told us if we helped them with this new casino, they would erase our debt."

"And by *help*, they meant threaten ranchers and burn down their barns?"

"Not in so many words."

"Why you two?"

"I don't know about me. I'm just a regular at the casino. Finn said they brought him in and comped him a room. Even gave him some chips to play with."

"Why do you think they did that?"

He shrugged.

I had a theory. Riverdale did background checks on all the ranchers in their expansion zone. They found out Jenn was married to Finn Rafferty, who was in town sniffing around last Thanksgiving. They targeted him to get his half of the ranch, but they needed some leverage. They made a gambler an offer he couldn't refuse to lure him into their extortion scheme. After that, Finn had nothing to lose. If he was successful, his debt would be forgiven, and he would walk away with at least some of the money from the sale. But things didn't work out the way they had planned.

The fact that Marty knew both Finn and Fishlips made him the closest thing I had to a lead in Finn's death and Jenn's kidnapping. I put on another pot of coffee.

"So you and Finn were working together?"

"Yes and no. He had his orders and I had mine, but we were working toward the same goal."

"Who burned down Hank Coleman's barn?"

"It wasn't me. That's all I know." He paused. "When they told me to torch the barn last night, I said no. Then I heard Finn was dead. I had no choice but to do what they told me."

"I guess it was lucky that I was there to stop you."

He shook his head. "I'm not seein' it that way."

"So you don't know who killed Finn?"

Another head shake. "If I had to guess, I'd say it was the guy with the lips, or maybe the other one."

I had to come up with another suspect besides myself. Vincent had seemed like the logical choice, but the whole point of setting Finn up was to get the ranch. Killing him seemed counterproductive.

Marty filled in some more details over another cup of coffee before I left him a little after three o'clock. I would have some explaining to do when Ziggy found him in the morning.

Chapter Twenty-Six

I walked into the station the next morning and smelled gasoline. Marty looked up at me from his cot in the holding cell.

Ruby's eyes flashed trouble as she whispered a warning. "I don't know what you did, but he's fit to be tied. He's been asking—"

"Bishop! In my office."

I can think of better ways to start the morning. I stuck my head into Ziggy's office. "Can I get a cup of coffee first?"

"Make it quick."

I poured a cup, thinking about what I would say. I should have been more prepared, but I was dead tired last night.

I sat on the edge of one of Ziggy's empty chairs and sipped my coffee.

"Who's in the cell?"

"His name's Marty Rogers. He tried to burn down John Stevens' barn last night."

Zig leaned back in his chair. "Keep talking."

"John asked me to stop by last night after the meeting so he didn't have a replay of the Coleman fire."

"And you didn't think to call me?"

"I figured you were busy with the Finn thing."

"About that..." He picked up some papers from his desk. "Close the door."

I obliged and returned to the edge of my seat. He handed me several papers, and I scanned them.

"Ballistics report says Finn's gun was the murder weapon."

I kept my nose in the papers. "That's good, right?"

Ziggy hesitated. "The problem is that your fingerprints were on it."

I swallowed hard. "I can explain that."

Ziggy waited.

I paused to consider how much to tell him. "About a week ago, I got a call from Jenn that Finn had showed up at the ranch. When I arrived, he had her by the arm. I didn't ask questions before I laid him out. He had a gun in his belt, and I took it from him. I released the clip and tossed them both into his car. That's the truth. You can ask Jenn."

"I will. But in this case, she's not exactly a credible witness."

"Are you calling her a liar?"

"No, Dillon. But you know how it looks, don't you?"

"I had nothing to do with this, and neither did Jenn."

"Let's give her a call."

"She's not home." I cursed myself for bringing up her name. Now I had to decide whether to let him in on the kidnapping, which might lead to the reason they were kidnapped in the first place.

"Where is she?"

I hesitated. "At her sister's."

Ziggy tilted his head and frowned. "I thought you told me she had three brothers."

"She does. It's... her sister-in-law. They're real close, you know, like sisters."

"Where does this sister-in-law live?" He pulled out a little pad and flipped it open.

"Oklahoma."

"I'll need Jenn's cell number." He put pen to paper and waited.

"She dropped it the other day. It's in the shop getting fixed."

"Do you have another number where I can reach her?"

"Uh... I don't."

He looked up and studied me through squinted eyes. I wouldn't have believed me, either.

"When was the last time you spoke to her?"

"Yesterday." The more you lie, the easier it is to get tripped up.

"When you talk to her again, tell her she needs to call me."

"Roger that."

"In the meantime... you're suspended. I'm going to need your gun and badge."

"C'mon, Zig. Don't do this. I'm not a killer."

"I'd like to believe that. In fact, I'm leaning in that direction, but this doesn't look good. I need to clear some things up first. I can't have a suspect—my only suspect at the moment—working the case."

I stood. He pointed to his desk, and I deposited my gun and badge there.

"Go home. If you're innocent, you've got nothing to worry about."

I would have believed that if I hadn't already been down that road back in Texas.

I hooked a thumb toward the holding cell. "You might want to talk to the guy in the cage."

***

Be careful what you wish for. I suddenly had all the time I needed to devote to getting Jenn and Alex back. Unfortunately, I would have to do it in street clothes, without the resources of the Teller County Sheriff's Department at my disposal.

I checked my phone for messages, wondering if the Whitehawks had located Jenn. Nothing. I couldn't remember if I had given them my phone number, and I'd never called them, so I had no way to contact them. Maybe Buck knew how to get in touch with them.

I found Buck near the round pen where they train the horses. He leaned against the fence, watching a couple of wranglers working with one of the horses.

I pulled up beside him and folded my arms over the top rail. "Is that Jacob Whitehawk?"

"He's real good with horses."

"I had no idea."

"His brother, too. It's in their blood. Hell, them two Indians was probably born on the back of a horse."

"Native Americans."

"What?"

"They're Native Americans."

"Whatever."

"Who's the other guy?"

"That's Randy." He turned his head away and spat a stream of tobacco juice into the dirt, then looked at me. "Turns out one of the new ranch hands knows somethin' about training horses."

"Good job, Buck."

He tilted his head. "I didn't teach him."

"But you hired him." I smiled. "I guess I made a good choice when I put you in charge of Human Resources."

He waved a dismissing hand. "Seth was pretty good at training horses, even when his heart wasn't into it. Since he's been gone, we haven't sold a single horse."

That couldn't be good for the bottom line.

Buck smiled and held up three fingers. "This month, we sold three, thanks to Jacob and Randy. That should make little Jenny happy."

"We need to find her first. That's why I'm here. Has Jacob or Jeremiah said anything?"

He shook his head. "Jeremiah's workin' on it."

"He doesn't have my number. Is he gonna send up smoke signals to let us know?"

"He's got my number."

That surprised me, given how poorly the three of them got along.

"Can I see your phone?" I asked. "I want to check in with him."

"I left it at the house," he said matter-of-factly.

"Then how do you know he hasn't called?"

"You asked if I heard from him, and I ain't heard nothin'."

We walked back to his place to check his phone. I looked around while he searched for it. I hadn't been inside since he moved back in.

Jenn's cousin, Seth, had fired him last year for embezzling from the ranch. Buck didn't strike me as the type that could spell embezzlement, let alone know how to pull it off. I think the real reason was that Buck was askin' too many questions about Roy's death. Buck packed up everything and left without saying goodbye. When Jenn found out, she was madder than a wet hen. She had some choice words for Seth, and I think that was the beginning of the end of their relationship.

Buck's record collection and Woodstock posters were back. I saw a new picture of him with Hattie that I probably wasn't supposed to see. The Whitehawk brothers' hardware store jokes at the bar the other night made sense now.

The shelf below Hattie's picture held several hand-carved wooden horses that stood about eight inches tall. The workmanship was stellar, and each one had a name carved into the base. I held one up when Buck entered the room. "Where'd you get these beauties?"

"I made 'em."

"Get out."

"Hand to God."

I nodded. "I'm impressed."

"There's one there for every horse I ever owned."

Every horse has their own personality. I could tell he'd captured them brilliantly. One of them looked familiar. I picked it up and read the name. "Romeo." I paused. "Is this Alex's horse?"

"You always do that? Snoop around people's houses?"

I set Romeo down. "I knew it. You gave Alex your horse when Apollo died."

He glared at me like I'd accused him of something awful, then handed me his phone. "Is this what you were after?"

The phone lit up and waited for a four-digit security code. I held it up. "Really, Buck?"

He grabbed it from my hand and tapped in the code. "I like my privacy."

"Can you just dial Jeremiah for me?"

He obliged and handed me the phone.

"Having any luck?" I asked when Jeremiah answered.

"I found the trailer. There's a black Chrysler parked out front."

He gave me the directions.

"I'll be there in fifteen."

When I turned to leave, I noticed something else I hadn't seen the last time—an antique pistol mounted on a polished wooden stand. I pointed to the pistol. "Is this the one they called the Peacemaker?"

He shook his head. "Peacemaker had the long barrel. That one there is the Sheriff's model."

"Where'd you get it?"

"Believe it or not, that there is the only pistol I've ever owned. Had my share of huntin' rifles, but never had a pistol until my daddy died. He was a snot-slingin' drunk, but he had a bodacious gun collection. He pawned most of 'em to buy his liquor, but Billy an' me each got one after he died."

"I didn't see it the last time I was here."

"I come across it when I moved. Thought it'd be nice to put it out."

"Did you ever shoot it?"

"Don't even know if it works."

I tossed Buck his phone. "Let's go for a ride."

"Sure." He hesitated. "You get the truck. I'll meet you outside."

The Silverado and Bronco were parked in front of the house. I headed toward the Bronco, then changed my mind. I was in enough trouble already. Ziggy took my gun and badge, but he'd forgotten about the patrol vehicle. I grabbed the portable police radio before I climbed into the Silverado and swung around to Buck's place.

I opened up the throttle on the way to Cripple Creek. I'd heard Ziggy on the police radio calling in a traffic stop in Victor—a black Chrysler 300, Wyoming plate number 2-602C. He was a good fifteen miles south of my position.

I found the turnoff that Jeremiah had described. We passed through a broken gate on a rusty old chain-link fence and found his Jeep parked in the bushes a quarter mile down a gravel road. I pulled in next to him, and we all got out.

Jeremiah pointed to a trailer fifty yards down the road, partially hidden by an old front-end loader and a pile of construction debris. The perfect place to stash a kidnap victim.

"Any activity?"

"A tall dude with no hair came out of the trailer and drove off right after you called."

Fishlips. "Nobody's been in or out since then?"

He shook his head.

I scanned the area and noticed train tracks that ran parallel to the road about two hundred yards from where we stood. Jenn and Alex had to be in that trailer.

"Did you get a plate number off the Chrysler?"

Jeremiah handed me a napkin with 2-602C written on it.

I told him to sit tight while Buck and I went back to my truck to figure out what to do.

"Ya think they're in there?" Buck asked.

"It makes sense." I pulled a pair of field glasses from under the seat and held them up to my eyes. "There's a padlock on the door."

"That old trailer's probably been abandoned for ten years. I can't think of any reason to lock it up."

"I can think of two, and I'm fixin' to get 'em out."

Ziggy's voice came over the radio again. He'd arrested an arson suspect after a routine traffic stop, and requested Bill meet him at the Cripple Creek station. Looks like Fishlips wouldn't be back any time soon.

"I'm goin' in," I said to Buck.

"What if the bald guy comes back?"

"He's not coming back." I turned to Buck. "Call me if anybody else shows up."

I grabbed a pair of bolt cutters from the toolbox in the back of the truck and ran toward the trailer. I snapped the lock and stepped inside to find Jenn and Alex tied to chairs at one end of the trailer. Jenn's eyeballs nearly shot out of her head. The tape over her mouth muffled her words beyond recognition.

I gently removed the tape, first from Jenn, then from Alex.

"How did you find us?"

"I had a little help. Are you okay?"

"I am now."

I looked at Alex. "How about you?"

He nodded.

I flipped open my pocketknife and cut the zip ties that bound their wrists. "We need to get out of here in a hurry."

"No argument here," Jenn said as I freed her legs.

When I stood up after freeing Alex, Jenn threw her arms around my neck. Alex hugged me from behind. My phone rang, and I freed up a hand to grab it. Buck's name appeared on the screen, and I shook my bad foot to stop the tingling sensation. This couldn't be good.

"What?"

"A black SUV just passed us on its way to the trailer."

Chapter Twenty-Seven

Vincent was back. I had my backup piece strapped to my ankle, but I hesitated to start a shootout with Jenn and Alex in the line of fire. If I didn't think of something else quick, I would have no choice.

"What's the matter?" Jenn asked.

"We've got company." I heard tires on gravel and pointed to the opposite end of the trailer. "Get down behind that desk."

I debated whether to throw open the door and come out guns blazing, or to lie in wait and blast him when he walked through the door. That's when it occurred to me he would know something was wrong as soon as he saw the busted lock.

I released my Glock 43 from its ankle holster and took a deep breath. A quick look at the other end of the trailer told me that Jenn and Alex were out of sight. I heard a car door open and close, then shouts. The next sound froze me where I stood. A gunshot. Then another. Then another.

I waited through a few seconds of silence before I opened the door a crack. I didn't know what to expect, but it wasn't what I saw when I stepped outside—Vincent facedown in the dirt, and Buck staring at his lifeless body from twenty feet away.

Buck held up his antique pistol. "Whatta ya know? It works."

A feeling of relief washed over me. Jenn and Alex were safe, and Vincent wouldn't be telling anyone about our little deal. Dead men don't talk. On the other hand, he was the most likely suspect—after yours truly—in the Finn Rafferty case. Him turning up dead might look a little too convenient in Ziggy's eyes.

Fishlips was in custody on an arson charge. He might also have been the shooter in Finn's motel room, but I had to be careful. Vincent could have shared the details of our arrangement with him. How else would he have known where Finn was staying?

I stared at Vincent's lifeless body. I needed to think.

"You're welcome," Buck said as Jeremiah came running down the road.

I looked up at Buck and nodded. Jeremiah stood next to Buck and patted him on the back like he'd just scored a touchdown.

"Shit!" I kicked Vincent's gun aside.

"It was self-defense."

I turned to Buck. "You mean when he saw a crazy old cowboy running toward him with a gun?"

Buck held up his left arm to reveal a hole in his bloodstained shirt sleeve. "He shot first."

Jeremiah nodded in agreement.

I shook my head slowly.

"What are we gonna do?" Buck asked.

"I need to think."

We had a few options. I didn't like any of them. Disposing of the body would just make things worse for everyone. Leaving it there for someone else to find wasn't much better.

Jenn stood in the doorway. "Dillon?"

"Don't let Alex see this."

She glanced back inside the trailer. "He's still under the desk."

"Keep him in there."

I looked at Buck's arm—just a flesh wound. "You'll live."

Buck hung his head and kicked at the dirt. "I know what you're going to say."

"You mean that I have to call this in?"

"Somethin' like that."

I exhaled sharply. "I'm probably in more trouble than you."

Buck placed his gun in my waiting hand. "I'd like that back when you're done with it. Sentimental reasons, you know?"

Jeremiah was the only witness. I told him not to go anywhere, then called Ziggy and gave him our location.

When I turned around, I found Jenn at my side, staring down at the body. "I think you should be with Alex."

"There's something I need to do first." She wound up and kicked the body so hard that it left the ground for a second before flopping back into place.

I pulled her back and wrapped my arms around her. "It's over now," I whispered. "He got what was coming to him, but this is a crime scene. Please go back inside and check on Alex. He needs you."

She wiped her eyes and nodded.

Buck had saved all of our lives, so my decision had not been an easy one, but it might be the only one I could live with. I'm not saying that there aren't times when rules should be bent, but even a man like Vincent doesn't deserve to be left out in the middle of nowhere for the vultures to pick his bones.

We would need to make the district attorney aware of the extenuating circumstances and hope he'd go easy on ol' Buck. I needed Ziggy to get on board, but that might be a tall order, given my current standing in the department and the kidnapping that I had so far failed to mention.

"Ziggy's going to be here in five minutes. You better get your story straight."

"Ain't no story."

"Okay, then tell me exactly what happened."

"I seen the car headed for the trailer an' knew you was in trouble. I ran over here an' told him to freeze, ya know, like the cops do. Then the sonovabitch shot me, so I let 'em have it. Twice."

I motioned for Jeremiah to join us. "What did you see?"

"After the car drove by," he said, "that crazy old man chased him down the road. The dead guy got out of his car and shot Buck, so he shot back."

Their stories matched, so I reckoned Buck probably had a chance, seeing he was trying to save our lives.

Ziggy pulled up and stepped out of his car. He put his hands on his hips and stared at Vincent lying in a puddle of blood. He turned his gaze toward me and his eyes burned a hole in my face. "What happened here?"

"It's a long story."

"I'm afraid you're going to have some real time on your hands, so let's start at the beginning."

Jenn appeared in the doorway, and Ziggy shook his head. "Let me guess. Sister-in-law's trailer?"

"I wish." I took a deep breath. "The dead guy kidnapped Jenn and Alex."

"And the hits just keep on coming..."

He pointed to Jeremiah. "What's he doing here?"

"Witness," I said.

"Please don't tell me you shot him, Dillon."

Buck raised his hand. "That would be me."

I held up the antique Colt, and Ziggy had me drop it into an evidence bag. "It was self-defense," I said. "He saved our lives."

Ziggy blew out a long breath. "Did anyone touch the body?"

I shook my head. I assumed he meant with their hands.

"We're going to have to sort all this out at the station after I get the coroner and CSU out here."

He excused himself to make some calls, and I checked on Jenn and Alex.

"What did you tell him?" Jenn asked.

I glanced at Alex. "The truth."

"What's going to happen to Buck?"

"I don't know. We're all going to the station to sort it out after the coroner gets here."

"Alex didn't see anything. He doesn't need to go."

"I'll talk to Zig. Maybe Hattie can pick him up at the station and take him home."

The coroner and a CSU tech arrived, and Ziggy huddled with them out of earshot. After a few minutes, they went to work. Ziggy put Buck in the back of his car and instructed the rest of us to follow him to the sheriff station in Divide.

With Alex in the back seat, we made it a point not to discuss what had just happened. Alex had a couple of questions when we got into the car, and I deferred to Jenn, who answered them better than I could have.

The cat was out of the bag about the kidnapping, and Ziggy would have a million questions. He would no doubt need to question Alex to corroborate our statements. Hopefully, we could take care of that first, so Alex could leave quickly.

Jenn called Hattie, who agreed to meet us at the station and take Alex home as soon as Ziggy would allow. He'd seen enough tragedy in his short time on this earth, and I silently berated myself for getting him involved.

When we arrived at the station, I told Ziggy that Hattie was on her way and asked if he could start his interrogation with Alex to spare him from spending any more time than necessary at the station. He agreed and ushered Alex into his office, then separated the rest of us to keep us from comparing notes. Poor Buck waited in the holding cell next to Marty.

Bill arrived a few minutes later. Apparently, Zig had called for backup to babysit while he questioned each of us separately. I asked him about the arrest in Victor, and he verified that a Carlo Kostas, aka Fishlips, was in custody in Cripple Creek. I wasn't sure if that was good news or bad.

Five minutes later, Alex emerged from Ziggy's office. When I asked if he was okay, he just nodded. I took his hand and walked him over to where Jenn and Hattie sat.

"Bishop. You're next." Ziggy motioned from his office door for me to join him. The look on his face reminded me of Pop when I tried to sneak in after curfew.

"I'm going to start with you, because you're supposed to be the grown-up here." He shuffled some papers on his desk, repositioned a microphone, and hit the record button. "I want you to start at the beginning and don't leave anything out this time."

The beginning? I couldn't remember where that was anymore.

CHAPTER TWENTY-EIGHT

In high school, I didn't enjoy writing essays. Too much work. You had to craft a beginning, middle, and end that flowed seamlessly, creating a logical and coherent story. I preferred multiple choice, or at least a direct question that could be answered in a few well-chosen words.

"I'm not sure where the beginning is," I said. "Can you just ask me what you want to know, and I'll tell you?"

He studied me for a moment. "Okay. When did this kidnapping take place?"

"Four days ago."

Ziggy let his head fall back against his chair and closed his eyes.

I waited.

He opened his eyes and leaned forward. "And you didn't mention this... why?"

I shifted in my chair. "It was stupid, I know, but I thought I could handle it."

"Or you didn't want me to know why he did it."

"There's that." I paused. "I think Finn was being blackmailed by Vincent. Finn owed him twenty-five grand and the interest kept piling on. The deal was that Finn could pay it off by helping secure the land Riverdale needed for the casino project. Jenn's land was at the top of his list."

"So, the dead guy you called in worked for Riverdale?"

I nodded, then hooked a thumb toward the door. "That guy, Marty, in the cage... he was in the same boat as Finn. Vincent and Fishlips were—"

"Who?"

"The guy you collared today on the arson charge."

The corners of his mouth curled up like he was going to smile, then snapped back. "So, Vincent and Carlo were working together as Riverdale enforcers?"

"Yes, until Finn got greedy and tried to take Jenn out so he could inherit the ranch. When that didn't work, he killed Kayla to cover his tracks. Riverdale was pissed and sent Vincent in to straighten Finn out. I'm not sure he was supposed to kill him, but when it went down, Vincent knew his days were numbered."

"Can you prove Vincent killed him?"

I shook my head. "So, he grabs up Jenn and Alex and holds them for the twenty-five-thousand dollars that Finn owed. You know, a peace offering to Riverdale to let him live."

"Why didn't you just tell me this four days ago?"

"He said no cops."

"You're a cop."

I shrugged. "I guess I don't count."

"How were you going to get the money?"

"It doesn't matter. I don't need it now, thanks to Buck."

"Let's talk about that."

"Jenn and Alex were being held in that trailer. I paid the Whitehawks to find them. Buck and I drove down there to meet up with Jeremiah. I didn't know Buck was carrying."

"What was your plan?"

"We didn't have one. I just knew I had to get them back."

"That was pretty stupid."

"It worked."

He waved a hand toward the door. "And now your friend is locked up."

"You've got to go easy on him. He saved all of our lives."

"Why don't you walk me through it?"

I closed my eyes and took a deep breath. "Jeremiah told us that Fishlips left the trailer shortly before we arrived. When I heard you picked him up in Victor, I knew he wasn't coming back any time soon. I broke into the trailer and freed Jenn and Alex, but before we could get out, Vincent rolled up."

I took another deep breath while Ziggy waited.

"That's when I heard three shots," I continued. "When I stepped outside, I saw Buck standing over him with a smoking gun."

"You didn't see him shoot?"

I shook my head. "Jeremiah did. He said Vincent fired first. Hit Buck in the arm."

"Is he alright?"

"Just a flesh wound, but I think you ought to have someone look at it."

"You could have just packed everybody up and left. Why did you call it in?"

I shrugged. "It was the right thing to do."

"I know. That's what puzzles me."

"Thanks for the vote of confidence."

"You've somehow been involved with every felony that's taken place in this county since you moved here, and I'm not sure that doing the right thing has always been your strongest motivation."

"Really? Then why did you hire me?"

"Okay. We're done here. There's a first aid kit in Ruby's desk. Go see if you can fix Buck up?"

"Roger that."

"And send Jenn in."

I told Jenn to relax and just tell the truth. With a hug and a kiss for luck, I sent her into Ziggy's office.

Ruby handed me the first aid kit and smiled at Buck. "Hey, Charlie."

Buck nodded and forced a smile.

"You two know each other?" I asked.

"Everybody 'round here knows Charlie." Ruby blushed.

I pulled Buck toward an empty chair. I sat him down and cleaned the wound with alcohol and applied a bandage. He made a hornet look cuddly as he watched, but I knew it had more to do with me than what I was doing. He had something he wanted to say, something I probably didn't want to hear.

I spoke first. "I don't know if I ever thanked you for saving our lives."

"Ya got a helluva way a showin' it."

"What was I supposed to do?"

He shrugged, like he knew I was right. Buck was a little rough around the edges and could probably start a fight in an empty room, but he struck me as a stand-up guy.

"I agree that you being locked up doesn't seem right, but I might be able to help with that."

"I'm all ears."

"Sounds like you're pretty popular around these parts."

"When ya live someplace your whole life, ya get to know a few people."

"I reckon we can use that to our advantage. We'll launch a preemptive strike. Get your case heard in the court of public opinion before it goes in front of a judge and jury. People around here will call you a hero."

"Ya think?"

"For sure. A regular guy like you standing up to the crook who kidnapped your boss and her eleven-year-old son. Throw in the fact that the dead guy was working for the big, bad casino company that's trying to take over their town, and you better wash your best shirt and shine your boots for when you're leading the parade down main street."

He waved a dismissing hand. "Aw, you're so full a shit."

"Okay, maybe I exaggerated a little, but I'm not wrong about you becoming a local hero of sorts."

"How's that gonna happen with me inside a cage?"

"Somebody just has to leak the story to the local paper."

"You'd do that for me?"

"I reckon I owe you one."

***

Ziggy released Buck on his own recognizance. I promised to take him back to the ranch and keep an eye on him. I think he was more worried about who would keep an eye on me. Ziggy still considered me a suspect in Finn's murder. I told him that was bullshit, and I think he wanted to believe it, but at the moment, I was the only one on his list. I needed to do something about that.

Jenn turned to me when we pulled out of the parking lot. "When were you going to tell me that Finn was dead?"

"We haven't had any time together since you've been back."

"Dillon, tell me you didn't do it."

"He didn't," Buck said. "It was a suicide."

"Sheriff seems to think you did it. Said your prints were on the gun."

"Don't you remember when Finn showed up at the ranch? After I decked him, I took his gun. You told Ziggy that, right?"

"I'm sorry. I forgot. I've been through a lot and my head's not right."

I slammed my fist on the steering wheel.

Jenn glared.

"If you tell him now, he's going to think I put you up to it."

"He might have thought that anyway."

She had a point. We rode the rest of the way in silence.

When we arrived at the ranch, we dropped Buck off and went into the house. Alex greeted us with Texas-size hugs as Hattie watched from the kitchen doorway. It was near dinnertime, and the house smelled like a restaurant. Mentioning something to Hattie was like issuing a press release, so, over dinner, I told her the story of how Buck saved our lives.

I thanked Hattie for stepping up again. After we said goodbye, we spent a family evening together so Alex could feel safe and loved. He pushed back a little at bedtime, so we let him stay up until he fell asleep on the sofa. I carried him up and tucked him in, then joined Jenn in our room.

I closed the door and stared at her as she changed for bed.

"Really, Dillon?"

I held my hands up. "I just want to talk."

She nodded her agreement and slipped under the covers. "What's going to happen to Buck?"

"I think he'll get off if Hattie has anything to say about it."

"She seemed pretty upset at dinner."

"I noticed."

"She didn't go home after she left here."

"Where did she go?"

"Buck's place."

I nodded. "I reckon there *is* something going on between the two of them."

"I told you. I know she's been lonely since Jim died."

I climbed into bed beside her. "And Buck's been carrying that torch for fifty years."

I turned out the light, held her in my arms, and said a prayer of gratitude for being able to do so again. After a few minutes of silence, I heard her sobbing and felt her tears on my chest.

"It's okay, Babe. You're safe now. I'm not going to let anything bad happen to you ever again."

Chapter Twenty-Nine

J enn gave Buck the following day off. Poor Buck didn't know what to do with himself. After watching him wandering around like a lost puppy, we invited him to join us for lunch at the local diner. Besides wanting to do something nice for the old coot, I thought it wouldn't hurt if some of the lunch crowd overheard us talking about the local hero who saved our lives.

I made it a point to stop and say hello to a couple of folks I recognized on the way to our table and encouraged Buck to do the same. After we were seated, I may have spoken a little too loudly when I told the waitress the reason for our lunch date.

Before our food even arrived, a couple of patrons stopped by our table to say hello to Buck and get some details. They asked to take a selfie with Buck, who politely declined. I nudged him and gave him a hard glare.

"Of course he would," I said and offered to take the picture.

My plan worked. By the end of our meal, Buck's heroics were the topic of conversation at every table.

News travels fast in a small town like Redfield. A reporter from the local paper greeted us when we arrived home after lunch. We all sat on the porch as she interviewed Buck. I helped him say all the right things and made sure he smiled for the pictures. The last shot had Jenn and Alex hugging the hero who'd saved their lives.

Ziggy would have something to say about my little PR stunt, but the way I saw it, I saved him a lot of paperwork, not to mention taxpayers' money.

***

There was plenty to do around the ranch to keep busy, but I had a killer to find, and I wouldn't find him there. My name was still the only one on Ziggy's list. I needed to convince him of my innocence despite the obvious motive and physical evidence to the contrary.

I planned to return to the scene of the crime and search for any clues that might have been missed. Coop had taught me a few things when we investigated Pop's death and Luke's disappearance back in Bradley. Perhaps this one wasn't even a crime scene. Proving a suicide, however unlikely it seemed, would provide me with the same get-out-of-jail-free card as finding a killer.

Jenn and I had agreed there would be no more secrets, so I told her my plan. She didn't like it, but she understood. She gave me a kiss and sent me off with her blessing.

I drove to the Golden Bear and parked in the corner of the lot, out of sight from the office. Room 117, still cordoned off with police tape, was visible from where I sat. I considered walking into the office and asking for the key, but it might be a tough sell in street clothes.

I stepped out onto the pavement and surveyed the entire scene. If I were Vincent, or Fishlips, or someone else here to whack Finn, this is where I would park. There were no lights nearby, so a vehicle parked there would be nearly invisible at night.

I wondered if CSU had looked around out here, or if they'd focused their efforts on the room. Here is where I would start, leaving no stone unturned. The immediate area around my truck held no clues. I widened the perimeter and found tire tracks in the dirt. Someone had misjudged the edge of the pavement as they backed into the farthest corner of the lot. Our killer, perhaps?

The front and rear passenger-side tires had compressed the soft earth, leaving a visible impression. Given the long wheelbase and the depth of the impressions, I would guess a full-size car or a truck. Coop once told me that the make of the vehicle could sometimes be determined by a tire's tread design. That didn't seem like something I would be able to do.

I compared the two imprints and found no tread pattern in the front, as if that tire had been bald. I took pictures, then estimated the size of the vehicle and scanned the area where the driver would have stepped out onto the pavement.

No dirt, so no footprints, but I found something peculiar. I brushed a small amount of a brown substance that had the consistency of shredded coconut into my hand and held it up to my nose. It smelled like horse shit with a touch of mint. It only took me a moment to remember where I'd smelled it before.

Buck, what have you done? My legs grew weak, and I leaned against my truck to steady myself. I should have been relieved to find a get-out-of-jail-free card, but this is not how I wanted it to go down. I tried to think of other reasons why Buck would have parked out there. Nothing came to mind. It had rained Saturday night, so the tire tracks couldn't have been left before then. Finn died Sunday.

I debated who to talk to first as I drove home. Jenn needed to know, but Buck deserved the benefit of the doubt before I jumped to conclusions. Jenn texted, asking when I would be home for dinner because Hattie had dropped off another meal. I parked in front of Buck's place and texted Jenn that I would be home in a half hour.

Buck answered the door with a bit of apprehension that I hadn't noticed before, but I hadn't been looking.

"Where's your truck?" I asked after he let me in.

"Still in the shop."

"Getting that tire fixed?"

He squinted one eye and studied me with the other. "That's part of it. Is that a problem?"

"I don't know."

Buck walked into the kitchen, and I waited. He returned with a bottle of whiskey and two glasses. He poured one and held the open bottle above the other as he waited. I didn't want a drink, but I probably needed one.

"Make it a double."

Buck nodded then poured.

"You ever been to the Golden Bear Inn?" I asked.

He handed me a glass, knocked his back, and poured another. After he ran the back of his hand across his mouth, he said, "Why? You lookin' for a recommendation?"

"I found some of your horseshit tobacco in the parking lot."

"Who says it's mine? Lotsa folks use that brand."

"I'm sure they do, but how many of them drive a truck with a bald front passenger tire?"

His expression hardened. "You got somethin' you wanna say?"

"Where were you Sunday night?"

He shook his head. "That damn truck's gonna be the death of me one way or another."

"Where were you?"

"I was havin' a few drinks with Jacob and Jeremiah. You seen me."

"You left early, if I recall. Where'd you go after that?"

"Sounds like you already know where I went." He poured a drink for himself and offered me another.

I declined.

"What did you do there?"

"I was fixin' to get those emails you wanted. Figured I could help you stay out of jail."

"What happened?"

His empty glass hit the table a little harder than the last time. "Nothin'. That's what happened."

"You got out of your truck."

"You try sittin' for an hour in a broken seat when your hemorrhoids is barkin' at ya."

"You were there for an hour?"

"More like an hour and a half. His car was parked outside. I waited to see if he might leave so I could sneak in and look around. I finally gave up and went home."

"No one entered or left the room while you were there?"

He shook his head. "After what you said at Hank's the night of the fire, I was just tryin' to help."

My shoulders relaxed. "I appreciate that."

"Ya gonna tell the sheriff?"

"I don't know yet." If Buck was telling the truth, his presence there was immaterial. "Have you told this to anyone else?"

He scratched at the stubble on his chin. "Hmm. Let me see..." He brought his hand down quickly. "Of course not! Why would I do a fool thing like that?"

"All right. Let's keep it that way."

"What are ya gonna do?" Buck asked.

"Those emails you tried to grab are in the evidence lock-up at the station. I want to know who Finn was talking to at

Riverdale. I'm running out of possible suspects. Maybe I can find one there."

"Anything I can do to help?"

"You've done enough. Just keep your mouth shut about that night, or we could both be in trouble. God knows I've got enough of that."

I left Buck's place feeling better, but only a little. Jenn didn't expect me home for another ten minutes, so I headed for the cabins.

Jeremiah answered the door.

"Can I come in?"

Jacob appeared behind his brother before they both stepped aside and let me in. "What's on your mind?" Jacob asked.

"Last Sunday when I saw you and Buck at the Wet Whistle, he left early. Did he say where he was going?"

They both shrugged.

I rolled my eyes. "I know he went down to the Golden Bear."

"Then why are you asking us?"

"Did he say why he was going there?"

They glanced at each other, then back to me. "He was looking for something," Jeremiah said.

"Something you told him you needed for a case," Jacob added. "He was trying to help you."

Sounds like Buck was telling the truth. "Did you see him again that night?"

Head shakes.

"Okay. Thanks."

***

The dinner Hattie had prepared for us really hit the spot. While Jenn cleaned up the kitchen, I helped Alex with his homework.

When he finished, we all watched TV together until he fell asleep on the sofa again.

"Can you do me a favor and keep an eye on Buck?" I asked in a low voice, so I wouldn't wake Alex.

"Why?"

"I had a talk with him earlier, after I found evidence that he'd been at the Golden Bear the night Finn was killed."

"You accused Buck of killing Finn?" Her voice was louder than Grandpa's Sunday tie.

I glanced at Alex, put my finger up to my lips, then whispered, "Not in so many words, but—"

She grabbed my arm and pulled me into the kitchen. "What's the matter with you?"

"He admitted he was there the night of the murder. He even got out of his truck."

"You think Buck could just gun him down like some wild-west outlaw?"

"You mean like he did to Vincent?"

For a moment, she had nothing to say. "That was different."

"He told me he was trying to help. Sound familiar?"

"Okay. I'm sorry I jumped all over your shit, but I don't think he killed Finn."

"I don't think he did either, I'm just sayin'..."

"Like Ziggy's just sayin'... that you did it? And he's got some pretty hard evidence. What do you have?"

She had a point.

CHAPTER THIRTY

I tossed and turned most of the night, thinking about the two suspects that remained—Vincent and Fishlips. One was dead, and the other was in jail, making it difficult to investigate either one. The ideal situation would be to find some hard evidence on the dead guy, who wasn't around to defend himself.

Perhaps I was going about this the wrong way. Instead of looking at suspects, what if I focused my efforts on the victim? Whatever Finn had gotten himself mixed up in got him killed. Buck had stuck his neck out to get Finn's emails, which could be the key to finding the real killer. I had a plan, but it would have to wait until nine o'clock.

After breakfast, I called the sheriff's office and waited for Ruby to pick up. "Don't say my name. It's Dillon."

"Sheriff's not here."

"Good. I need to see the CSU report from the motel."

"I don't know, Dillon."

"Please, Aunt Ruby. I need to know what they have, so I don't get sent away for something I didn't do." I paused. "You believe I'm innocent, don't you?"

Silence hung in the air for a moment. "I believe you, but it doesn't look good."

"You've seen the report?"

"I may have glanced at it when I typed up the sheriff's notes and filed everything."

"I need a copy. Can you do that for me?"

More silence. "You know I think the world of you, Dillon, but—"

"Ruby, please. Nobody has to know. I need everything you've got. I'll come by when he's not around and pick it up."

"Well... okay. He's out of the office for the next hour. It's now or never. Use the back door in case he comes back early."

"I'm on my way."

Ruby met me at the back door with a folder in her hand.

"Thanks. I owe you."

"Big time," she said with a nervous smile. "Be careful."

Ziggy might have shown up at any moment, so I tossed the file in the passenger seat and left in a hurry. I parked in the empty lot of the burger joint where I took Jenn for her first meal after being released from the county jail last year.

I rolled the window down a couple of inches and picked up the folder. Ziggy's notes were on top, so I scanned through them. Two new names, both Riverdale employees, stood out. I flipped through Finn's emails, looking for the ones Zig had referenced in his notes.

It appeared Finn had been running out of time. A few veiled threats were made, but nothing that would stand up in court. Vincent was mentioned in one of the emails by a man named Rudolph Ruger, who might have been his boss. My guess was that Fishlips reported to him as well.

Finn's main objective was to acquire Jenn's ranch by any means possible. If his failure was a death sentence, Vincent or Fishlips seemed to be the logical choice for executioner. Sadly, I was no further along than I was an hour ago. I called Brickman and made arrangements to get the file to him. He told me he had both Marty and Fishlips in his custody.

When I got home, Jenn announced that she'd sold the south 300 acres. The farmer she'd been talking with had upped his offer to $1700 per acre. Mort was drawing up a contract that included a clause restricting the resale of the land for twenty-five years. She had also asked him to apply for a business license, and help her create a business plan for the new riding center. She had a meeting set for Monday with a contractor to go over the architectural plans Roy had drawn up. I hoped I would be around to see it completed.

If I didn't find a plausible suspect, or at least uncover some promising leads, Ziggy would have no choice but to arrest me and let a jury sort it out. Given the available jury pool, I reckoned I'd have a better than fifty-fifty chance, as more of the locals were against the casino coming in. If word got out that Finn had been working against them on behalf of the casino, my odds would surely improve.

"Earth to Dillon..." Jenn placed her hands on her hips. "Are y'all listening to me?"

I hadn't seen Jenn this excited for some time. "Sorry, Babe. That's great news."

"Because it was a private sale, I figure we'll clear about half a mil. That should be more than enough to build the new indoor arena, a conference center with classrooms and a mess hall, and hire a manager to oversee the day-to-day operation. Someday we'll add more cabins for extended visits, but for now we'll only offer day services."

I gave her a big hug and told her how proud I was that she was on her way to honoring her uncle's dream. This called for a celebration. I grabbed a bottle of whiskey and two shot glasses from the cabinet, and we toasted Jenn's achievement. It went down easy, so I poured two more. We knocked them back. I poured another round.

"I'm good," Jenn said as she held up her hands.

I drank both.

Alcohol has a tendency to amplify whatever you're feeling at the time. It became obvious that she was on her way to the moon, while I was headed for a place so low I'd have to look up to see hell. Perhaps I should've found a different way to celebrate.

"I think y'all have had enough for one morning."

I was just getting started. "You're probably right." I capped the bottle, not wanting to spoil her moment any more than I already had.

"I have to talk to Hattie about getting the proper permits." She took the whiskey bottle from my hand. "Why don't you come with me, and afterwards you can buy me lunch at the Bluebird."

***

Hattie walked Jenn through the permit application and assured her she'd have no trouble getting approved for such a worthwhile project. She said the town council would welcome the distraction from the hotly contested casino vote they would soon have to make.

My mind was somewhere else, so I let Jenn do the talking. As I sat quietly and watched the two women chat over the paperwork, it occurred to me I had overlooked a group of possible suspects—the landowners who refused to sell. One stood out. Hank Coleman had lost his barn, and Finn either lit the match or was otherwise involved. I needed to find out if Hank had an alibi.

We stopped at the Bluebird on the way home for the lunch Jenn invited me to buy her. It was the least I could do. I must have zoned out again after we'd been seated.

"Care to join me for lunch?"

I looked at her, a little embarrassed. "I'm sorry."

"You look like the cheese fell off your cracker. What's bothering you?"

"I've been doing some investigating on my own and coming up with a whole lot of nothing. The only shred of evidence I found points to Buck."

The waitress brought us some iced tea.

"Buck again? Leave the poor man alone. He was there because of something you told him. He was just trying to help. Besides, he said he didn't do it."

I shrugged.

"Shame on you for getting him involved."

"I didn't tell him to go there."

"Maybe not, but Buck's always been a loyal employee… and friend. If he can find a way to help, he's going to do it."

"Roger that."

After a brief glare, she smiled. "Wait. Why are we here?" She paused. "Oh, yeah, because I raised enough money to begin work on the riding center."

She held up her glass, and I tapped it with mine. "I'm proud of you, Babe. And I'm sure Uncle Roy is, too."

We spent the rest of the time discussing her plans, but not much was mentioned about where I might fit in. For that matter, she never mentioned her role in the enterprise going forward.

"So, where do we fit into all of this?"

She hesitated, then took a drink of tea. She set the glass down and her expression became serious. "Here's the thing Dillon…"

I braced myself. That was like starting a sentence with, "We need to talk." Nothing good ever followed those four words.

"These plans... they're Uncle Roy's dream, not mine."

I waited for more.

"I'm not sure I even want to stay in Colorado."

It's a good thing I was sitting down. "I thought you loved ranching."

"I do, but these plans take it to a whole other level. It's a lot of pressure. I thought I could do it, but now I'm not so sure."

"I never knew you to run away from anything."

She frowned. "I'm not running away, Dillon. I came out here because I love being around horses, and I have a lot of great memories here. But mostly I came here to honor a promise I made to Uncle Roy on his deathbed. That's what I'm doing now."

"And after that?"

"It'll be time for a new chapter, I reckon."

"What about me?" I swallowed hard. "You're not thinking of—"

"Leaving y'all behind?" She smiled one of her beautiful smiles. "I've got plans for you, cowboy."

My stomach, which had bottomed out, snapped back into place.

CHAPTER THIRTY-ONE

I drove to the sheriff's station after I dropped Jenn off at the ranch. Our lunch conversation caught me off guard. Given the way she'd talked about the ranch before we left Texas, I just figured Colorado would be our forever home. Now I wasn't so sure. That would be fine by me. We've had nothing but trouble since we moved there, but truth be told, Texas hadn't been much better.

I wouldn't mind being closer to Mama and Coop, but I didn't want to get my hopes up. It was unlikely that Jenn would consider moving back to Bradley while Nicole was living there, but there were plenty of small towns where we could land and still be close to family and friends.

Ruby watched with wide eyes as I walked through the front door. I paused to look at the empty holding cell before walking into Ziggy's office.

"If you're here to talk about the investigation, you can turn right around and—"

"Hi, Dillon," I said with a heavy dose of sarcasm. I continued, "Hi, Zig. How are you doing? Not bad. How about yourself?"

Ziggy rolled his eyes.

"Where's the prisoner?" I asked.

"Transferred. State Police picked him up an hour ago."

I guess it was time to call Brickman.

Ziggy frowned. "I heard you were sniffing around the crime scene."

"I may have stopped by to take a look. You chased me away the first time."

"You've been suspended. Please don't interfere with this. I'm trying to run an investigation here."

"I have more than a little skin in the game, so forgive me if I'm doing the same." I blew out a long breath. "When are you going to talk to Jenn again? She'll tell you how my fingerprints got on Finn's gun."

"I'll talk to her, but she's emotionally involved. Her testimony isn't going to hold much weight."

"Have you looked into any of the other landowners? Hank Coleman had as much motive as I did. Have you at least talked to him?"

"I'm doing the best I can, given my limited resources."

"Yeah, too bad you suspended your best deputy. I heard he was a pretty good investigator. Solved a major case last year before it went cold."

Ziggy glared at me. "I'm just following protocol."

"And I'm just following this overwhelming urge I have to stay out of jail for something I didn't do."

"We're on the same side here."

I stood. "Why doesn't it feel like it?"

"I'm trying, Dillon," he said as I headed for the door.

"Talk to Hank, or I will," I called over my shoulder.

I tipped my hat to Ruby on the way out, and she forced a smile. When I reached my truck, I climbed in and called Brickman.

"I've got good news and bad," he said.

"Give me the bad first."

"Kostas has a strong alibi. I don't think he could have killed Rafferty."

If Vincent didn't pull the trigger—and we didn't know that yet for a fact—I would have bet money that Fishlips did it.

"He claims Courtemanche was with him, but we haven't been able to verify that."

I pounded the dash. I had hoped to pin it on one of them. Vincent might still be an option unless someone could corroborate Fishlips's story.

"What's the good news?"

"The other guy, Rogers, agreed to a deal and gave up the name of Courtemanche's boss back in Wyoming. His name is Rudolph Ruger. You ever hear of him?"

I didn't want to screw up Marty's deal. I felt sorry for him. He was a victim in Riverdale's underhanded scheme—a stupid victim perhaps, but a victim nonetheless. "I just recently came across that name in some email messages from Rafferty. They obviously knew each other."

"Interesting..."

"I hope you didn't mention my name when you transferred them from county." I was sure I would have heard about it by now if he had.

"I kept you out of it. I told Sheriff Scott that both Kostas and Rogers were tied to an interstate investigation and asked him to let us know of any more Wyoming connections he might come across."

"I appreciate that. The sheriff loses his vertical hold when it comes to me."

"I'll keep that in mind."

***

I woke up Monday morning feeling like I was on a mission. The final Riverdale meeting was scheduled for seven o'clock that night, and I planned to be there to cause a scene. Riverdale Gaming had blood on their hands, and I planned to hold them up for everyone to see. I had nothing to lose. Jenn disagreed. She believed I would put an even bigger target on my back than the one that was already there.

A bigger target might be what I needed to draw out Finn's killer. It might also be what this town needed to shut down Riverdale's expansion so things around here could get back to normal. Most of the councilors would be there, as well as ranchers and landowners from both sides.

The day went by quickly as I prepared my case and gathered my evidence. I would need to get the most damaging testimony out quickly before Riverdale shut me down. Jenn agreed to accompany me for moral support.

"I just want to apologize in advance," I said to Ziggy on the way in.

"What are you planning to do?"

"Tell the truth."

"According to Dillon Bishop."

"All I can do is present the evidence." I made a sweeping motion with my arm toward the gathering crowd. "And let the jury decide."

Ziggy removed his hat and ran his hand back through his hair. He knew it was what this town needed.

"I'll go peacefully," I said. "All I ask is that you take your time when they ask you to throw me out."

Ziggy studied me for a moment, and I thought it could go either way. He glanced at Jenn by my side before nodding his approval.

When the meeting started, Ziggy positioned himself on the opposite side of the room. As soon as they opened up the floor, I stood and let loose a searing commentary on Riverdale's methods of intimidation. When I waved Finn's emails above my head and named names, Ziggy got the nod to remove me from the proceedings.

He made his way slowly to my position, allowing me time to continue. Two-thirds of the crowd cheered when I mentioned the local hero who saved Jenn and Alex's lives after one of Riverdale's enforcers had pulled them from our truck at gunpoint and kidnapped them. The cheers turned to boos as Ziggy led me to the door.

"Well, how'd I do?" I asked when we got outside.

"Officially, no comment. Unofficially, you've got a huge set of *cojones*."

Jenn joined us.

"Hank's in there," I said to Ziggy. "You should talk to him."

"Go home," Ziggy said. "I need to get back inside before they kill each other."

Several councilors met him at the door and huddled there.

We sat in my truck and waited for the meeting to end. The doors opened and folks swarmed out of the building like hornets from a burning nest. I'd stirred the pot, alright. Ziggy and Bill followed and shooed away anyone who lingered, looking for trouble. When the coast was clear, they escorted the Riverdale folks to their cars.

"I thought I told you to leave," Ziggy said as he approached my truck.

"What did Hank say?"

"He denies having anything to do with Finn's murder, but he doesn't have an alibi."

"And then there were two."

Chapter Thirty-Two

I had a hunch that Hank Coleman was another victim of circumstances, and as innocent as I was. When I returned to the Golden Bear for another unsanctioned look around, I planned to look for clues left behind by a third suspect. If I uncovered evidence that pointed to Hank, so be it. I've been known to have a misguided hunch or two.

I parked in the same spot in the back corner of the lot. The police tape fluttered in the breeze around the entrance to room 117. I didn't think I'd have much luck getting the key from the manager, but I also didn't want to add breaking and entering to my list of criminal charges.

The manager looked up from behind the counter when I walked in. "It isn't every day we have local celebrities walk through our door."

I turned around to see if someone important had followed me in.

He smiled. "You're that deputy from the meeting last night. Bishop, right?"

I would take advantage of my new celebrity. "That's me. You can call me Dillon." I held out my hand.

"Where's your uniform?" he asked, looking me over as he shook my hand.

"Day off."

He nodded. "You need to get into 117?"

"I do, as a matter of fact."

He pulled a key from a rack on the wall behind him and handed it to me. "Just so you know. I run a tight ship. Never had so much as a broken pinky toe around here until last week."

"Has anyone been in the room since then?"

"Oh, no. Sheriff said not to let anybody in there." He paused. "Present company excluded, I'm sure."

"Absolutely."

"Do you know when they'll be finished?" He scrunched up his face. "That yellow tape is bad for business."

I nodded. "I'll see what I can do."

I ducked under the tape, unlocked the door, and slipped inside Room 117. Without the benefit of a crime scene kit, I couldn't dust for prints or take samples. After almost an hour, I conceded I wouldn't find anything that CSU had missed. I left the room and locked up, disappointed.

On my way back to the motel office, I noticed an old man smoking a cigarette in front of one of the other rooms. He watched me from his chair, tilted back against the wall.

"I know who you are," he said as I approached.

"You do?"

His rail-thin body swam in his flannel shirt, and I wondered how he kept the back of his chair pinned against the wall. A cowboy hat sat low on his forehead as if his bushy gray eyebrows were the only thing that kept it from sliding down over his face. Like his dusty old hat, this poor fellow had seen better days.

"You's the one who caused all that ruckus at the meetin' last night."

"Guilty as charged."

"You live on that big ranch up the road where Bucky Owens works."

"You know Buck?"

"We go back farther than you been walkin' around on two feet, I reckon."

"That's a long time." I paused. "Maybe you can help me out."

"I can try."

"You sit out here a lot?"

"Every chance I get. Livin' in a dinky motel room isn't for the faint of heart."

I gestured toward room 117. "Were you out here the night that the man died over there?"

"Sure was."

"Did you see anything out of the ordinary?"

"I suppose Bucky runnin' out of that room like his tail was on fire would be considered out of the ordinary."

"Wait. You saw Buck coming out of room 117?"

He leaned forward until the front of his chair hit the pavement, then crushed out his cigarette under his boot. "The only reason I'm tellin' you this," he said, as he stood toe to toe with me, our faces six inches apart, "is 'cause you strike me as the kinda fella who'll give ol' Bucky a fair shake."

"Did you tell any of this to the sheriff?"

"He didn't ask."

Buck lied to me. We were gonna have us another conversation. I shook the man's bony hand and thanked him for his honesty.

"What did you say your name was?"

"I didn't."

I waited.

"Most folks just call me Curly."

***

Buck lied to me. What was worse, I believed him. I was so mad I could've chewed up nails and spit out a barbed wire fence. My foot pinned the accelerator to the floor as I raced back to the ranch.

I drove past the house and skidded to a stop in front of Buck's place. No one answered when I pounded on the door. After I checked the barn and stables, I marched over to the house.

"Where's Buck?" I asked after I threw open the door.

A smile slid off Jenn's face. "I don't know."

"I need to find him."

Jenn's hands rested on her hips. "Y'all come bustin' in here without so much as a proper greeting or a kiss on the cheek..."

I took a deep breath to give my blood pressure a chance to drop. "I'm sorry," I said as I kissed her cheek.

"That's better." She gave me another moment to calm down. "I'm glad you're here. We need to talk."

"About what?"

"The future."

My pressure rose again. "We may not have a future if I don't find out why Buck's been lying to me."

"What are you talking about?"

"Buck told me he went to Finn's motel that night, but he insisted he never went inside. But I have an eyewitness who saw him running out of Finn's room. Why would he lie about that unless he was covering something up? And why was he running?"

"Who saw him?"

"An old friend of his who lives at the motel."

"Buck's not home now?"

"No. I was just over there. I checked the barn and the stables, too."

"I suppose you would have walked in guns blazin' like you always do."

"What's that supposed to mean?"

"You need to dial it back a little. You'll get a lot further if you start off with conversation instead of an accusation."

"I have an eyewitness that—"

"And the sheriff has your fingerprints on the murder weapon."

She had a point. "Okay. I'll just talk to him. But if I don't find out what really happened that night, there won't be any future for us to discuss. You realize that, don't you?"

"I'm aware." She rubbed her arms as if they were cold. "But I find it hard to believe that Buck could kill someone."

"What if it comes down to him or me?"

She hesitated.

"Really? You have to think about it?"

"I'm on your side, Dillon. Always will be."

***

Buck never came home that night. The next morning, I caught up with one of the ranch hands feeding the horses. He said he hadn't seen Buck yet, which was unusual. I saw no sign of his truck, but I couldn't remember if he'd gotten it back from the shop yet.

My stomach bottomed out. I wasn't sure if I was worried about Buck, or worried that a likely suspect had flown the coop. Then it occurred to me that ol' Buck might have been riding in the bedroom rodeo at Hattie's last night.

I walked back to the house, where the smell of breakfast sausage greeted me at the door.

"Buck's gone," I said when I found Jenn in the kitchen.

"What do you mean he's gone?" She shut off the stove and turned around.

"Nobody's seen him this morning. I don't think he came home last night."

She frowned. "That's SO not like him."

"I had a crazy thought. What if Johnny and June were knocking boots over at Hattie's last night and lost track of time? Maybe they're still asleep."

"I don't know. Buck's been waking up at the crack of dawn for the last fifty years." She tilted her head. "Maybe he knows that you know."

"Not a chance. Unless his friend Curly told him." I shook my head. "But why would he do that?"

"Maybe he figured it would be better coming from him than you."

"I'm not sure why he even told me in the first place."

"Some people just can't keep a secret." She shooed me away with both hands. "Go get washed up and tell Alex breakfast is almost ready."

"Alex. Breakfast," I called from the bottom of the stairs, then dialed Hattie's number.

"I need to talk to Buck. Have you seen him?"

"Uh… Buck? Can't say that I have." She paused. "Is everything alright?"

"I don't know. That's why I need to talk to him."

"Sounds serious."

"If you see him, tell him to call me."

"Will do."

Chapter Thirty-Three

Jenn sat down at the computer after breakfast.

"What are you working on?"

"The town council meets tomorrow, and I'm preparing a presentation about the Equine Therapy Center."

"I thought you already had the permits you need."

"I do, but this is the last meeting before they vote on the casino, and I want to show them that we can put the land around here to better use. I think this project will bring new money into the area and still maintain the integrity of the land."

"A lot of the interested landowners on both sides will be there."

"And I'm going to show them how they can prosper from this, as well."

"Sounds like you've got the solution to everyone's problems."

Her shoulders slumped. "Except yours."

The solution to my current predicament continued to elude me. I'd made some inroads with Ziggy, thanks to Jenn corroborating my story about the gun, but it didn't hold as much sway as an impartial witness. The recent revelation about Buck could help my case, but it came with a whole other set of problems. None of that would matter if I didn't find him.

A car pulled up in front of the house, and I went to the window. Brickman got out and walked toward the door. I hoped for good news, but braced myself for the worst, even though, as far as I knew, he wasn't involved with the Rafferty investigation.

His expression was unreadable when I met him at the door.

"So, what brings you by?"

"Just a little business to discuss."

Still nothing. We sat in the living room and Jenn joined us. Alex was busy upstairs with his video games.

"I have some good news on the Riverdale front. Grand Jury handed down indictments for Ruger and Kostas. They'll be prosecuted. Courtemanche, Rafferty, and Kayla Green would be too if they were still alive. The information you provided played a big part in securing the indictments."

"Glad I could help."

"Who knows about this?" Jenn asked.

"It'll be announced later this week, but I thought you should know now in case you planned to attend the council meeting tomorrow night."

"Do you want us to say something at the meeting?"

"I can't answer that," he said as he smiled and nodded his head.

Message received. "Roger that."

"I plan to give a brief presentation about the Equine Therapy Center we're gonna build here at the ranch. It was my Uncle Roy's dream to name it after his deceased fiancée, Asha White-hawk."

"I heard about the accident. I'm sorry. It's a wonderful thing you're doing, and the town should welcome it with open arms."

"At least half of them," I said.

Brickman smiled. "I don't think you have to worry about the other half. I wouldn't be surprised if, when this goes public, Riverdale pulls out."

"That would be great."

"Speaking of news..." Brickman turned his attention to me. "When you called me, you failed to mention that you were the prime suspect in the Rafferty investigation. What's that about?"

I shook my head. "A misunderstanding. Some circumstantial evidence and a motive, but I didn't do it. The coroner's preliminary report called it a suicide, but the sheriff seems to think otherwise."

"I see. Well, don't be afraid to call if you need help with anything."

Mentioning Buck at this point didn't seem like a good idea.

***

The council meeting was standing room only. After being ejected from the meeting on Monday, I let Jenn take the reins tonight. She had the crowd in the palm of her hand as she handled her presentation like a pro. The fireworks didn't start until after the presentation, when she mentioned that they had indicted several Riverdale employees for kidnapping, extortion, and murder. She vowed to keep her land out of the hands of such thugs and implored everyone there to do the same.

One outspoken proponent of the casino asked her how she knew about these alleged crimes. A hush fell over the room when she replied in a shaky voice that she and her eleven-year-old son had been kidnapped and held for ransom by these men less than two weeks ago. She went on to mention how Deputy Bishop and a local hero, Charlie "Buck" Owens, rescued them and probably saved their lives.

I appreciated the shameless plug, but after talking to Curly, I wondered if Buck's hero reputation might be a little tarnished. Nevertheless, Jenn did her job in holding Riverdale's nefarious practices up to the light.

The Riverdale representatives didn't wait for the meeting to be adjourned before slithering out of the room. Outside, I stood back and watched the line of people waiting to congratulate Jenn and wish her well.

"You must be proud," Ziggy said from behind me.

I turned. "She did a great job with her presentation."

"I'm talking about what she said afterwards." He glanced toward the crowd that had gathered around her. "If I didn't know better, I'd say she had a pair as big as yours."

I laughed. "You don't want to be on the wrong side when she gets fired up."

After a few moments of silence, I said, "Are you sure you want to be seen talking to a known fugitive?"

He smiled and shrugged before his expression became serious. "How did you know about the indictments?"

I debated whether or not to mention Brickman's name. "Don't forget, I used to be one of your best investigators."

"We miss you at the station."

"You can always reinstate me."

"I think you should know that we've all but eliminated Hank as a suspect."

"How's that?"

"CSU found some prints at the scene that they haven't been able to identify. Hank's prints were not a match."

"I don't suppose you found any of mine there?"

"Only on the gun."

"What about the cleaning staff?"

"We ruled out all the employees."

"So you're not going to arrest me?"

"Not yet."

The crowd around Jenn thinned out. "In that case, I should probably get going."

"Don't leave town," Ziggy said.

We laughed. I think he was half serious.

***

Hattie called on the way home from the meeting.

"Hi, Dillon. It's about Buck."

"Is he okay?"

"I'll leave that up to you."

I didn't know what that meant. "Do you know where he is?"

"Why don't you just come over to the house?"

"I'll be right there."

I told Jenn to call the sitter and tell her we would be late, then banged a hard U-turn and headed for Hattie's place.

Hattie ushered us into the kitchen where Buck sat at the table sipping something from a coffee mug.

"Have a seat," she said. "Can I get you anything?"

I glanced at Buck, who'd been silent since we arrived. "Just an explanation."

"Buck's been here with me the last two nights."

"Why didn't you say something?" Jenn said. "We were concerned when you didn't show up for work."

"I'm sorry about that, but I didn't know what to say. I didn't want to hurt you."

"Your leaving hurt us. We've been worried sick."

"First let me apologize," Hattie said. "I lied to you yesterday, Dillon, and I'm sorry. I needed time to figure things out."

"I lied, too," Buck said, "But you already know that."

I glanced at Jenn. She'd been right. Buck knew that I knew. "Tell me what happened. The truth this time."

"Am I talking to a deputy or a friend?"

I didn't realize that he thought of me as a friend. "It shouldn't matter, but I'm here as a friend."

"I was in the room when that damn fool died."

Jenn's eyes grew wide, and she covered her mouth with her hand.

"Did you shoot him?" I asked.

"Not exactly."

"What does that mean?"

"I didn't pull the trigger." He held his cup up and looked at Hattie. Can I get some more?"

"Just coffee this time."

He waved a dismissing hand. "Forget it."

"Let's start at the beginning," I said.

Buck inhaled and looked around the table. "I thought I could break into his room and steal them papers you was looking for."

"Just to be clear, you're talking about Finn Rafferty's room at the Golden Bear?"

He nodded.

"What happened when you got there?"

"I didn't see his car, but I waited a spell to make sure no one was there. When I went inside and turned on the light, he was sleepin' in the bed. He pulled a gun and took a shot at me. It missed, and I rushed him before he could get a second one off."

That explained the bullet hole near the door. So far, everything lined up.

Buck held up his cup again and looked at Hattie with desperate eyes. "I could really use somethin' besides coffee."

Hattie gave in and poured some bourbon into his cup.

"Then what happened?" Jenn asked.

"I drove him right into the headboard and we wrestled over that gun. He tried aimin' it at me, and I pushed it right back. I was thinkin' what a damn fool I was for goin' over there in the first place. Then I heard a noise that sounded more like a firecracker in a tin can than a gunshot. That's when he stopped movin'."

Silence descended on the room as Buck stopped to take a drink.

"Bullet went in under his chin and blew the top of his head off."

"That must have been awful," Jenn said.

"Awful for him, I reckon. I was grateful to still be breathin', even though I thought I might be deaf in one ear."

Hattie looked like she was about to burst into tears. She loved this old goat, and I felt her pain.

"What did you do after that?"

"I panicked. I never intended to kill no one." He stopped for another drink. "I stood and looked at the mess. I'd never seen no one kill themselves, but I imagined this is what it would look like. The gun was layin' in his lap, so I grabbed my work gloves from my pocket and laid the gun in his hand."

"Probably should have left it where it was." I said. "If he did kill himself, the recoil would have knocked it out of his hand."

Buck glared. "I musta missed that episode of *CSI*."

"Just sayin'..."

Jenn kicked me under the table.

"Do you realize the position this puts me in?" I said.

"Yeah, 'cause it's all about you," Buck said under his breath.

"Buck." Hattie's voice was stern. "Be nice. Dillon and Jenn are here to help."

"It's about both of us, Buck. I could go down for this, even though I didn't do anything."

"Buck knows that. He came over here to talk me into running away with him."

"You were gonna run?"

"I was fixin' to leave a note behind sayin' what I did."

"What happened to the Buck who offered to kill Rafferty when he threatened to take Alex away? I recall him saying he was an old man with nothing much to live for."

"That was then," he said.

"And this is now," Hattie added as she placed her hand on the table. A diamond sparkled on her ring finger.

Jenn took her hand and examined the ring. "Aww." Her face lit up like we weren't in the middle of a life-or-death conversation. "Congratulations. I'm so happy for y'all."

Hattie shined for a moment. "Buck bought me this ring forty years ago. Never had the nerve to give it to me until now."

Jenn turned to Buck. "Is that true?"

He gave a silent nod.

Jenn gave me another kick under the table, and a look like I should congratulate the happy couple. I hadn't yet recovered from the shock of the announcement.

"Jeezus, Buck!"

"What he means is congratulations." Jenn smiled on my behalf.

"Am I the only one who sees a problem here?"

No one responded.

I took a deep breath to collect myself and consider the ramifications of this new development. Buck had just dragged poor Hattie into his mess—precisely why Jenn's ring was buried in a dresser drawer and not on her finger until I cleared my name. "I honestly don't know what to say."

CHAPTER THIRTY-FOUR

Jenn raised an eyebrow. "What are our options?"

"They're not good. Either I turn Buck in, and we hope for the best, or I end up on trial for something I didn't do."

Jenn and Hattie looked at each other. I didn't want to think about what might be going through their minds.

"Or we leave a note sayin' what happened and disappear for good. Nobody has to go to jail."

I said nothing as I looked around the table.

"Which one's it gonna be?" Buck asked.

I ran my fingers back through my hair and sighed. "I don't think I can just look the other way, Buck."

"Sure you can," Hattie said.

Buck looked at me. "Why don't you two just go home and forget this meetin' ever happened?"

I locked eyes with Buck, and for the first time, I noticed how scared and tired he looked. Buck never showed much emotion, and it had taken a toll.

"We'll be gone in the morning," he continued. "We'll tell Ziggy to come by so he can find the note."

I turned to Hattie. "And you're okay with this?"

She played with the ring on her finger. "Maybe."

Jenn leaned in over the table. "What about your children... and the store?"

"I don't know." Tears rolled down Hattie's cheeks.

"Who's gonna attend y'all's wedding? I certainly wouldn't want to miss that, and neither would Dillon."

"Damn it, Buck," Hattie said between tears. "Why'd you have to go looking for trouble, you old fool?"

He hung his head. When he raised it again, his bushy mustache couldn't hide his trembling bottom lip.

Jenn pleaded, "There's got to be another way."

"If there is, I sure don't know it."

"It was an accident, for God's sake, not cold-blooded murder." Buck let out a heavy sigh as he rubbed the back of his neck. "I ain't no criminal."

Hattie looked at me, her eyes filling up. "Please, Dillon. Don't say anything to Ziggy just yet. Give us one more night together. Whatever you decide to do, you can do it in the morning."

I reckoned it wouldn't hurt. It would buy me some time to decide how to proceed. When I took the oath, I swore not to betray my integrity, my character, or the public trust. That seemed like a tall order given the current situation.

I thought about my little brother, the one we called Lawman Luke, the one who was going to clean up the county when he grew up. But he never got a chance to grow up. In his ten-year-old mind, there had been only black and white. At some point, we all realize that there are many shades of gray in between.

Buck didn't do anything wrong except break into that room. He didn't go there to kill Finn, and he didn't pull the trigger. I wanted to believe a jury would see it the same way. There had to be a way out of this where neither of us ended up in jail.

I stood. "C'mon, Jenn. We need to go."

Hattie looked up. "Does that mean you'll—"

"I'll see you in the morning."

***

"The construction crew plans to break ground tomorrow," Jenn said, presumably to avoid any more talk about Buck, at least for the ride home.

"That was fast."

"Should be substantially complete in three months. That's what they told me."

I forced a smile. "That's exciting."

We rode the rest of the way in silence.

When we got back to the ranch, Jenn paid the babysitter, and I drove her home.

"Did I do something wrong?" the sitter asked after we drove in silence for a few minutes.

"What? No, not at all. I'm sorry, I just have a lot on my mind."

"That's a relief." She paused. "I thought you would be excited about the good news."

"What good news?"

"They're not going to build the casino. The permit applications were withdrawn."

"Who told you that?"

"My dad. He's on the town council."

I dropped her off and raced home. I called out to Jenn as soon as I walked through the door.

"Shhh! You'll wake Alex up."

"You did it."

She tilted her head. "Did what?"

"The casino. They withdrew their application. They're backing down."

"Where'd you hear that?"

"Maggie."

"The babysitter? How did—"

"Her father's on the council."

"That's great, but y'all did more than me to scare them away."

"It doesn't matter. They're not a threat anymore. Things can get back to normal around here."

"I hate to be a Debbie Downer, but we're nowhere near normal yet." Jenn sighed. "What are y'all going to do about Buck?"

"I haven't decided yet."

"They look so cute together, don't they?"

"Cute is not a word I would use to describe Buck."

"You know what I mean. They're finally together after all these years."

"If you're asking me to keep quiet about this, I can't do that. Besides, who do you think is going to jail if Buck doesn't come forward?"

"Did you kill Finn?"

"I can't believe you would even ask me that."

"Just answer the question."

"No. I did not kill him."

"Then y'all got nothin' to worry about."

"Maybe in a perfect world, but we both know that's not the case. Innocent men go to jail all the time."

"This isn't Bradley, Texas."

"I know, but I don't want to take that chance again. I don't want to risk losing you and Alex. You know how much I want a family. I missed out on that growing up."

"I know it's hard for you to do. There's a lot of bad history, but maybe you can have a little faith in the justice system. It's not like Harley Wilkerson is the sheriff."

I snorted. "If Harley was sheriff of Redfield, I'd have been gone faster than a prairie fire with a tailwind."

"Lucky for me he's not." She kissed my cheek and headed for the stairs. "Y'all coming to bed? We've got a big day tomorrow."

"I'm going to make a cup of tea first."

***

The tea I drank before bed saved me from a long night of tossing and turning. I woke up refreshed and knowing what I had to do. Jenn might not like the consequences of my decision, but she would agree with my motivation.

I had grown to despise the F-word. *Family*. Mine had been taken from me, and revenge had hung like a dark cloud over much of my life. Things were different now. I vowed not to perpetuate the lies and corruption that had contributed to my disdain.

Jenn had renewed my faith in that word. I stared down the barrel of having a family of my own, and I no longer feared the outcome. But the decision to turn Buck in was more about telling the truth than saving myself. Black and white. Truth and lies. Lawman Luke would be proud.

Once Buck was in custody, and he told *his* truth, hopefully black and white would melt into softer shades of gray. Finn's death was an accident. Buck didn't pull the trigger. I believed others would see that and judge accordingly.

Jenn was not in bed when I awoke. Everything in the house rattled, and I looked out the window as an excavator and two large dump trucks rolled past the front of the house. Jenn would be right there supervising when they reached the construction site.

I got Alex ready for school and waited with him at the bus stop. He begged for me to let him stay home and watch the heavy equipment tear up the ground. I assured him they would still be there when he got back and reminded him that tomorrow was Saturday. He gave a defeated nod and hung his head. I held out my fist, and he gave it a half-hearted tap.

After Alex reluctantly stepped onto the bus, I returned to the house to find Jenn waiting on the front porch swing.

"Sorry I wasn't around to get Alex ready for school, but—"

"No worries. The hard part was getting him on that bus when there's an excavator tearin' up his backyard."

She smiled before her expression fell. "How y'all holding up?"

"I'd rather hug a rosebush than face the rest of this day." I sat beside her, and silence filled the next few moments. "We missed you at breakfast."

"I apologize for runnin' out on y'all like that, but I had to make sure they dug the hole in the right place."

"We managed."

"It appeared that way... at least until I got a look at the kitchen." She stood. "I better go take care of that."

"I should quit stalling and go do what I gotta to do."

Jenn wished me luck. I kissed her goodbye and headed for Hattie's house.

I felt relief when I saw that Buck's truck was the only vehicle in the driveway. Hattie must have left for work. Might be best to do this without her around.

I knocked on the door. No answer. I knocked again. It wasn't a stretch to think that Buck was inside sleeping off a bender. The third time, I pounded a little harder. I didn't like how this looked. I tried Buck's phone, then Hattie's. No answer.

I drove to the hardware store and found the door locked. Two customers waited in their cars in the parking lot. I checked the time—after nine. It wasn't like Hattie to be late.

CHAPTER THIRTY-FIVE

I dialed Jenn from my truck.

"They're gone."

"What do you mean, gone?"

"I mean no one answered at the house, and the store is locked up. I think they're on the run."

"Oh, Dillon, I can't believe they would just—" Jenn paused. "Hattie's truck just pulled up, and Buck's with her."

"They're at the house?"

"Walking up to the door as we speak."

"I'm on my way. Don't let them leave."

I raced home and took the porch steps two at a time. I found the three of them having coffee like it was just another day.

"I thought you two—"

"Snuck out of town like thieves in the night?" Hattie said.

I shrugged. "Something like that."

Hattie straightened in her chair. "I called Ziggy. He's on his way."

"How did you know that's what I decided?"

"It's the right thing to do. Buck isn't a killer. We'll take our chances with a jury."

"We may not have to," I said. "I think your boy, Ziggy, will listen to reason."

"He won't break any rules, if that's what you mean."

"He doesn't have to break them, maybe just bend them a little."

Hattie glanced at me, then looked away.

I cocked my head and stared at her. "I think that's why you're here. Ziggy doesn't know you two are engaged, does he?"

She hesitated. "No, he doesn't. Am I that transparent?"

"You're his mother. You want him to have all the facts, especially if there's a possibility of shifting the odds in your favor."

"I don't think Buck deserves to go to jail over this."

Jenn placed a hand on Hattie's arm. "None of us do."

I turned to Buck. "You just need to relax and tell the truth."

"I *am* relaxed."

His eyes told me otherwise.

A car pulled up outside. I met Ziggy at the door and ushered him into the kitchen. He removed his hat, and we engaged in the usual pleasantries. I offered him a seat next to Buck. Once seated, he scanned our little group with curious eyes that stopped on his mother, sitting across the table. "You said you have something to tell me?"

Without a word, she held her hand out over the table and gently wiggled her fingers, causing the light to reflect favorably off her diamond.

Zig's eyes widened, and his mouth fell open.

"Say something."

"Is that what I think it is?"

"Only if you think your mama's gettin' hitched again."

"Isn't it wonderful?" Jenn said.

"I'm happy for you, Mama." He paused. "Who's the lucky fella?"

Buck gave a little wave to get Ziggy's attention. "That would be me."

"Seriously?"

I suddenly realized that this plan of Hattie's could backfire. If Ziggy didn't approve of his new stepfather, he could blow it up by sending Buck to prison for the next twenty years.

"You knew that Charlie and I had been friends since we were kids." She paused and a flicker of a smile crossed her lips. "What you didn't know was that he bought me this ring forty years ago. I wasn't ready to settle down back then. He was smart enough to realize that."

Ziggy shifted in his chair. "I suspected there was more to that story."

"This doesn't take anything away from your father," Hattie said. "We had a wonderful life together, and you and Raven and Jimmy are a testament to our love."

"I think it's sweet," Jenn said, "that you held on to it for all these years."

"I reckon I was holdin' on to the hope that I might get to use it someday." Buck's eyes got a little misty.

Ziggy turned and extended his hand. "Welcome to the family, Buck."

Buck forced a smile and shook his hand. I wished for everyone's sake this moment could have taken place under different circumstances.

"Who else knows?" Ziggy asked.

"No one outside this room." Hattie looked like she was about to burst into tears.

"What's the matter, Mom?"

I took a deep breath and straightened in my chair. "There's more to the story."

Ziggy tilted his head and raised an eyebrow.

I hesitated.

"What?" Ziggy stared at his mother. "You're not pregnant, are you?"

Despite the tension in the room, we all laughed.

"Oh, baby, that ship sailed a long time ago."

Ziggy blew out his relief.

I reckoned after he heard what I was about to say, he would rather deal with a pregnancy.

"There's more."

Ziggy smiled and held up his hands. "I think I've had enough surprises for one day."

I straightened in my chair and placed my hands on the table. "Ziggy!"

He flinched, and the smile slid off his face.

"I need you to listen carefully. It's the reason you're here."

He studied me, his expression a mixture of fear and curiosity.

"It's about Finn's death." I'm sure that for a moment he half expected me to confess. "Buck was in the room when Finn died."

An awkward silence hung in the air as Ziggy stared at me, apparently struggling to wrap his head around what I'd just said.

"Maybe Buck should tell you what happened."

Buck cleared his throat. "Like I told Dillon, it was an accident."

"An accident? What did you mean to do?"

"He was helping me out," I said.

Zig turned to me. "So you knew about this?"

"No. Of course not. I went back to the scene and found a couple of things in the parking lot that led me to believe Buck was there that night. When I questioned him, he admitted he was."

Ziggy pulled out a pen and his little notepad.

I took the pen from him. "Just listen."

"I knew Dillon was in trouble, so I was fixin' to get them emails he told me might help him."

"So you went to Finn's hotel room? We didn't know where he was staying. How did you?"

"Jacob and Jeremiah Whitehawk found him for me."

Buck told Ziggy exactly what he'd told me, that he was surprised to find Finn sleeping in the room. Finn took a shot at Buck, who rushed him before he could get off another. The gun discharged while they struggled, and Finn was killed instantly.

"That's the God's honest truth," Buck said. "I didn't pull that trigger."

Silence fell as Ziggy stared at Buck for a moment before closing his eyes.

Hattie spoke first. "Say something, dear."

Ziggy looked around the table at each of us, then blew out a breath. "You've put me in an awkward position."

"Maybe not as awkward as you think." I took this opportunity to make a case for him to go easy on Buck. I knew he would want to play this by the book, so I pointed out a few things he might not yet have considered. "The coroner's preliminary report called it a suicide, right?"

"Yes, but there were some inconsistencies. The bullet in the wall near the door, for example."

"Let's pretend we don't know how that got there. Isn't it possible Finn's gun could have discharged some other time when he was cleaning it?" I didn't wait for an answer. "He could have gotten drunk one night and fired off a round in his room. The gun had a silencer, no one would've heard it. Or maybe he wasn't drunk. Maybe Vincent or Fishlips paid him an unexpected visit."

"It's possible."

"There's no upside to punishing Buck. Just sign off on the coroner's report, and we can put all this behind us. Besides, think of all the money you can save the county by avoiding a trial that Buck is going to win, anyway."

"Can you prove Buck was there that night?"

"Can you prove he wasn't?"

"This all sounds too convenient. Almost like you're covering something up."

I shook my head, disappointed that he could still think I had something to do with this. "What can we do to prove it to you?" Ironically, most suspects had to prove they were not at the scene of a crime, but Ziggy was making us prove Buck *was* there.

"What if I told you I had an eyewitness who could place Buck at the crime scene that night?"

"I'll need to talk to him."

I hoped Curly would be as forthcoming with Ziggy as he'd been with me. "His name is Curly Stenshorn, and he lives at the Golden Bear."

I glanced at Buck. He nodded, and I knew that Curly had told him about our conversation.

"I have one set of prints that I haven't been able to identify," Ziggy said after a moment of silent deliberation. "If you're willing to let me take your prints and they match the unidentified prints from the crime scene, *and* this witness corroborates your story, I'll consider it."

"Knock yourself out," Buck said.

"I have a portable fingerprint kit in the car. I'll get it, and we can do it right here. Tomorrow is Saturday, so we won't have the results until Monday, but we can get things started right now."

It would make for a long weekend, but I reckoned we had no choice.

When Ziggy left the room. I turned to Buck. "What are the chances those are your prints?"

"We knocked over the night table, and I righted it before I left, but by then I'd put on my work gloves."

"Did you put on the gloves before you went inside?"

He shook his head. "No reason to until he shot himself, and I moved the gun."

"So, your prints should be on the doorknob."

"Don't see why not."

Ziggy returned and took a full set of Buck's prints. The mood in the room was upbeat, like maybe there was a light at the end of this long tunnel. Ziggy appeared to be as hopeful as the rest of us that this would be resolved quickly in our favor.

Ziggy said his goodbyes and left the room. Hattie followed.

"We did the right thing here." I patted Buck on the shoulder. "Everything will work out."

"I'm gonna hold you to it."

Hattie gave her son a kiss goodbye at the door.

All we could do was wait.

CHAPTER THIRTY-SIX

I spent most of Saturday with Jenn and Alex, watching the land being cleared for the 60-by-120-foot pole barn that would become the indoor riding arena. It was the perfect distraction from an otherwise unbearable waiting game.

I had done my best to show Ziggy what I felt was the most practical resolution of an impractical situation. There was considerably more at stake here than the bizarre events of that ill-fated night. All of our futures hung in the balance, waiting on Ziggy's final decision.

Jenn was playing with Alex while she kept an eye on the construction, and I thought about how lucky I was. I knew now that she was my forever girl. I wanted to make it official, especially after seeing someone like Buck take the leap. He seized the day, and I admired that. He obviously had a bigger pair than me.

Mama once told me that people make their own destiny. Perhaps that's what I needed to do here, and I had a pretty good idea how to do it.

I asked Jenn and Alex if they would like to take Sunday afternoon off from all our troubles and go on a picnic. Alex responded with an enthusiastic yes, then asked what a picnic was. Jenn explained and agreed it was a wonderful idea.

At noon on Sunday, we loaded Jenn's Bronco and headed north. I was sure Jenn had a pretty good idea where we were headed. Alex had never been there. We drove for ten minutes before I pulled over next to three rocks that looked like giant teeth that had grown out of the ground.

"We're on foot from here," I said.

We hauled all our picnic gear along a dirt trail that disappeared between two of the teeth. Eventually, we reached a clearing that sat at the edge of a cliff, high above a river that snaked its way between jagged red rock and rolling, evergreen-studded hills. Majestic snow-capped mountains guarded the land below on two sides, creating a breathtaking vista.

Jenn pointed to the top of the highest mountain. "Look, Alex. That's Pikes Peak."

His eyes were wide with wonder, and he reminded me of myself the first time Jenn brought me here.

"What do you think, pardner?" I had no words the first time I looked out on God's creation, so I didn't expect an answer. "This is my favorite place in the whole wide world."

"Is this where we have our picnic?"

"It sure is," Jenn said. "Help me get set up."

The first time I'd seen this place was in a dream back in Texas. I had never been to Colorado, but apparently Leotie, the medicine woman, had. The night she died, she stopped on her way to heaven to show me this place and to say goodbye. Imagine my utter amazement and disbelief when I moved to Colorado and Jenn brought me here to see her favorite place on the entire six-hundred-acre ranch. It had been an otherworldly experience, and I believed this place possessed some sort of spiritual power that connected not only our lives, but our very souls. I saw it as an appropriate venue for what I had planned for the afternoon.

The three of us sat on a blanket and enjoyed food and beverages from a large picnic basket, our cares melting away into the magnificence that surrounded us.

After lunch, I pointed to the woods. "If you'll excuse us, Alex and I are going to use that bathroom over there."

"Don't forget to wash your hands."

I smiled and led Alex toward the trees.

"Do you have to pee?" I asked, once we were out of earshot.

Alex shook his head.

"Okay. Neither do I." I put on a serious face. "I brought you over here because I need to ask you a very important question."

He cocked his head. "Really? What is it?"

I knelt on one knee and looked him in the eyes." "I would like to ask your permission to marry your mama."

After a moment of silence, Alex squealed like a schoolgirl.

"Man up, pardner."

Alex gave me his best tough guy look. I studied him for a moment. Oh well, it was a start.

"What's going on over there?" Jenn called.

Before I could respond, Alex replied.

"Pop wants to know if—"

I put my hand over his mouth. "Shhh... it's our secret."

He nodded, and a smile crossed his lips.

"Dillon?" Jenn called again. "Is everything okay?"

I placed both hands on Alex's little shoulders. "So, what's it going to be?"

"That would make me very, very happy."

"We're good," I said over my shoulder.

"Are you going to be my pop for real now?"

A tear tried to escape, and I pushed it back with a smile. "That's the plan."

He lunged at me and wrapped his arms around my neck, nearly knocking me to the ground. The tear made another attempt to break free.

I extricated myself and hooked a thumb in Jenn's direction. "When we go back, let me do the talking."

He nodded and held out his fist. I smiled and gave it a bump before we made our way back to the picnic.

When we returned to the blanket, I offered Jenn my hand and helped her to her feet as Alex sat. I turned and winked at him. We took a few steps toward the edge of the cliff and looked out over the canyon below.

"This place holds special meaning in my heart, as I'm sure it does yours. I feel it somehow connects us. Because of that spiritual connection, and many more reasons, I love you very much, Jenn, and I want to spend the rest of my life with you."

Jenn's eyes grew wide, like she knew what was coming next. She glanced at Alex.

I reached into my pocket, then dropped to one knee. Alex clapped. I turned to him and whispered, "Not yet."

Jenn giggled.

I opened the little black box that I'd been holding on to for too long and held it between us. "Jennifer Lee Myles, will you marry me and make me the happiest man on earth?"

She brought her hands up to her mouth, and a shred of doubt crept into my mind. *What was she waiting for? Say yes, Babe, say yes.*

"Dillon Bishop, I would be honored to be y'all's wife."

I glanced at Alex and gave a quick nod. "Okay, now."

Alex clapped as I kissed my new bride-to-be and took a giant leap into the rest of my life.

Chapter Thirty-Seven

Alex talked for the entire ten-minute ride home about having a proper family. You'd think it was Christmas morning, and he'd just unwrapped a box full of puppies. We'd never told him about the adoption problem, and now there was no need to crush his spirit. Finn was gone. Problem solved.

I hadn't really thought about where or when we would get married, but sooner sounded better than later. When we returned home, Alex ran up to his room to draw some new pictures for the fridge.

"So, when do we start planning this shindig?" I asked.

"Seriously? I've been planning this ever since y'all moved in."

"You're kidding, right?"

"Well, in my mind, anyway."

I sat on the sofa and patted the cushion next to me. "Tell me what you got."

"I don't need a fancy wedding. I want it to be small—just a few friends and family. We can have it here on the ranch, and we don't need to spend a lot of money. I did the big wedding once, and look how that turned out. It's more about marrying the right person than hosting some elaborate affair."

"You're preaching to the choir." I looked down at my feet. "I'm fixin' to buy me some new boots and maybe a sport jacket."

"You can wear dungarees if you like, as long as they're clean."

I raised an eyebrow. "So, when do you want to do this?"

"I don't know. Maybe June or July. The construction should be finished by then. We could christen the new meetin' room. It'll hold forty or fifty people, and it's right next to the kitchen."

"I think the Bluebird does catering."

"All we need to do is pick a date."

"We'll need to see when Mama and Coop can come out. I plan to ask Coop to be my best man."

Jenn's expression fell. "I don't have a maid of honor."

An awkward silence settled in. "You haven't known Jolene for very long, but she really likes you, and I'm sure she'd be honored to stand with you."

"You think?"

"For sure." I pulled out my phone. "We can do that face thing on the phone and ask them."

Jenn smiled, biting her lower lip as she did. "This is really happening, isn't it?"

I nodded and leaned in for a big hug. "I have an idea," I said as we disengaged. "We could have a double wedding here at the ranch with Hattie and Buck."

My suggestion produced another awkward silence.

"Or not. It was just an idea."

She hesitated before her face lit up. "Just a *great* idea."

Pop used to say, if everything is coming your way, you're in the wrong lane. I hoped that wasn't the case here. Ziggy could still throw a monkey wrench into our plans, but I wouldn't know anything until tomorrow. There was nothing I could do about that today except fill my head with positive thoughts. Today we would celebrate our engagement. Tomorrow, God willing, we would celebrate some more.

***

I helped Buck with chores on Monday morning to make the time pass quicker. I followed him through the stables with a couple of hay bales in a wheelbarrow.

"How was your weekend?" I asked.

"About the same as yours, I reckon." He pulled a couple flakes from a bale and dropped them into one of the stalls. "Ya gonna call the sheriff?"

"He won't know anything until at least this afternoon."

"You best keep busy until then."

"Tell me something I *don't* know."

"There's plenty to do around here."

That was an understatement. Buck kept me busy until well after lunch. At three o'clock, I called Ziggy.

"Did you hear anything about the prints?"

"Not yet." He paused. "You're not worried, are you?"

"Why should I be? I didn't do anything wrong. I'm a little concerned that Buck might get jammed up. You don't want to see that happen, do you?"

"I don't. But I'm going to run this by the DA."

"Do you think that's a good idea?"

"I think it's what I need to do."

"Once you tell him what happened, there's no going back."

"I'm aware, but I don't want the truth to come out in the future, and have him lay the blame in my lap. I have a career to consider." He paused. "Besides, I can be very persuasive."

"I'm sure you can, but—"

"Dillon. I need to get him on board."

I reckoned if I was in his shoes, I would do the same. "Sounds like you've made up your mind."

"I know the DA. He's a friend of the family. I'm not saying that will have anything to do with his decision, but I've known him a long time, and he's a stand-up guy."

"Okay, just please let me know what you guys decide as soon as possible."

"Will do. How's Buck holding up?"

"About how you'd expect. Your mama's a strong woman, but I think this is giving her a run for her money."

"How long have you known about the two of them?"

"Hattie showed us the ring the night before you saw it." After a brief silence, I said, "Are you okay with that?"

"Sure, as long as he makes her happy."

"I proposed to Jenn over the weekend, and she said yes."

"What?" He paused. "Are you serious?"

"You can bet the farm on it."

"That's great. I'm happy for both of you."

I stopped short of telling him we might move back to Texas. "Nobody else knows, so do me a favor and keep it under your hat."

It had been a long day. I felt like one wheel down and my axle dragging, but I needed to stay busy. I went inside to check on Jenn. She'd spent most of the day cleaning the house and finding little jobs to keep herself busy. Alex was back from school, so I let him teach me how to play his new Avengers video game. I had a hard time keeping up, but he was real patient.

I lost track of time until the phone rang an hour later. I left Alex's room, and Jenn met me in the hall.

"Hey, Zig."

"Dillon, I need to ask you an important question."

I glanced at Jenn. "Sure."

"When are you coming back to work?"

"Really?"

"I can sure use another set of hands around here."

"Does that mean…?"

"I talked with Curly, and he corroborated your story."

"And the prints?"

"They matched. The DA is okay with ruling Finn's death a suicide."

I lost my words for a moment.

"Are you there?"

"Still here." I paused. "That's great news."

Jenn covered her mouth with one hand to keep from screaming, while slapping my shoulder with the other.

"So, when are you coming in to pick up your gun and badge?"

I held up my hand and stepped back out of Jenn's reach. "I'll have to get back to you on that."

"Get back to him on what?" Jenn whispered.

I ended the call. "He wants me to come back to work."

Her smile slowly receded. "Is that all? I thought maybe—"

"That, and… it's over. Finn's death is officially a suicide. Buck and I are off the hook."

Jenn jumped into my arms, knocking my phone to the ground. I would have followed it, had I not taken a half step back to brace myself. She squealed and hugged my neck.

Alex appeared in his bedroom doorway and watched us for a moment. "What's the matter?"

"Mama's very happy," Jenn said, still holding on.

He tilted his head. "About getting married?"

Her eyes met mine. "Yes, baby, about getting married."

Chapter Thirty-Eight

I felt like a prize turkey on the day after Thanksgiving. "This calls for a celebration."

"What y'all have in mind?"

"How about we invite Hattie and Buck over for some steaks and beer? We can celebrate the present and talk about the future."

"Do you think they know?"

"Ziggy didn't say. If they don't know yet, they're gonna find out when they get here."

"I hope they don't. I want us to tell them."

"Only one way to find out. You call Hattie, and I'll call Buck. We don't say anything about a celebration, got it?"

Jenn nodded as she tapped the numbers on her phone.

If Buck or Hattie knew anything, they didn't let on. They agreed to break bread with us, but I imagined they considered it their last supper.

Hattie and Buck showed up together with solemn expressions. A smile flashed across Hattie's face when we greeted them. Buck nodded, looking resigned to whatever might come. I could tell they hadn't talked to Ziggy yet.

I brought drinks for everyone, and we sat in the living room.

"I have good news and good news." I smiled. "Which do you want first?"

They looked at me with puzzled expressions. "Either one, I guess," Hattie said.

I glanced at Jenn, who could barely hold back a smile. "The good news is that Ziggy signed off on the coroner's report. It's over. We can all get on with our lives."

Jenn squealed.

"When did he tell you that?" Buck asked after a long draw on his beer.

"He called this afternoon to see when I was coming back to work."

"And he told you they wasn't pressin' any charges?"

"Sure as I'm sittin' here drinkin' a cold one."

Buck slumped down in his chair like someone had just deboned him. Hattie reached out and took his hand. They exchanged a look.

"What's the other good news?" Hattie asked with a smile as sweet as stolen honey.

"I'll let Jenn show you."

She held out her left hand in front of Hattie's face. Both girls squealed. Buck looked at me. His mustache twitched, and he nodded.

Hattie shook her head. "That's about as much good news as I can handle in one day."

I asked if anyone needed another drink before Jenn and I excused ourselves to make dinner. I returned to the living room a few minutes later, beer in each hand, to find Hattie and Buck making out like a couple of high school seniors after the prom.

"You two need a room?"

"After we eat," Buck said.

My mind conjured up a picture I reckoned I'd never be able to unsee. I delivered their drinks and stepped outside to fire up the grill. When I went back inside to get the steaks, Hattie was in the kitchen with Jenn. Buck followed me outside.

I knew I should keep my mouth shut, but I needed to tell someone to make it real. "Don't say anything to anyone yet, but Jenn and I are moving back to Texas."

Buck stared at me with one eye closed, then took a drink.

"Well? Say something."

"Mama taught us if we ain't got nothin' good to say, to keep our big yaps shut."

I flipped the steaks, then looked at him. "I know there's somethin' that resembles a heart inside that carcass of yours. Would it kill you to say you were going to miss us?"

He waved a dismissing hand. "Ahhh."

I handed him the barbecue fork. "Keep an eye on the steaks while I run inside for a minute."

When I returned with a platter, he was poking at one of them.

"I think they're done," he said when he saw me.

"Good. The girls are ready inside."

Jenn called Alex down from upstairs, and we all took our seats. At the end of our prayer, I added a bit of gratitude for all that had transpired in our favor over the weekend. A resounding "Amen" followed from all in attendance.

We took our time with our food and lingered around the table when we'd finished.

"Jenn and I were thinking... since we're all gettin' hitched, maybe we can do it together."

Hattie blinked back her surprise. "You mean like a double wedding?"

"If that's okay with you. We could do it right here on the ranch."

"We thought maybe at the end of June," Jenn said. "The construction should be complete by then. We can have the reception in the new building."

Hattie looked at Buck, who shrugged. She turned to me. "That means he'd love to, and I second the motion."

"I waited this long," Buck added. "A few more months won't matter, I reckon."

Alex looked around the table and smiled. I'm not sure he understood what was going on, other than he was getting a proper family.

Buck finished his beer and set the bottle on the table. "Is that before or after you move back to Texas?"

I glared at Buck as Jenn's eyes burned a hole in the side of my face. I noticed Hattie didn't look too surprised, which led me to believe that Jenn had spilled her beans about the same time I was spilling mine. Fortunately, we'd already spoken with Alex about moving, so he wouldn't be hearing it for the first time from Uncle Buck.

"We're going to miss you," Hattie said.

I looked at Buck. "We?"

He shrugged.

After we said goodbye to Hattie and Buck and cleaned up the kitchen, I asked Jenn to show me that face call thing so I could see Mama's face when I told her.

"Dillon. What a delightful surprise."

I held the phone out a little farther so Jenn could get in the picture.

"Hey, Missus B. How y'all been?"

"We've been fine, dear. How are you two getting on?"

"That's why I called," I said. "You'd better sit down, because I've got a couple more surprises."

Her eyes blinked a couple of times. "You know I'm not good with surprises."

"You're gonna like this one, Mama. Jenn and I are getting hitched in June."

Mama placed her hand on her chest, and I thought she might burst into tears.

Mort's head appeared at the edge of the screen. "Congratulations to both of you."

When Mama regained her composure, she wished us the same.

"And we might need someplace to stay while we look for a new place to live."

She wore a puzzled look. "You're moving off the ranch?"

"Do you think you can put us up for a couple of months?"

"Here with us?" The puzzled look lingered. "I don't understand."

"We've decided to move back to Texas."

The tears she'd hidden a few moments ago were now in full view. "Mort," she called. "They're moving back home."

His head appeared again. "That's great news. When?"

"Not sure yet. Sometime later this year."

"Sounds good. Let me know what I can do to help you get settled."

"Dillon, you have no idea how much this means to me." Mama wiped her tears.

I was pretty sure I did.

***

Ziggy called the following day when he heard I might be leaving Colorado. He brought up my reinstatement again, and I promptly resigned. There were no hard feelings, I just needed to spend more time with my family and help Jenn with the plans for the riding center. And then there was the whole wedding thing.

The next three months would be very busy. Near the top of the to-do list was hiring staff that could run the center in our absence. Jenn would oversee the operations remotely and visit from time to time, but we needed boots on the ground in Colorado to manage the day-to-day activities. We also needed to hire a licensed equine therapist.

As with any startup, there wasn't a lot of money for salaries, and we would need a good deal of it to hire a well-qualified therapist. So, Jenn and I came up with the perfect solution for who should run the place.

Someone once told me there wasn't a leaf that blew on this ranch that he didn't know about. While I figured it was at least part bullshit, Buck had been ranch foreman since before I was born. Of course, we still needed someone to keep an eye on him and keep him sober. That's where Hattie came in.

We couldn't pay them much in the way of salaries, so we sweetened the deal by offering to let them live on the ranch in the homestead that we would vacate when we moved. It was a sweet deal, and they wasted no time accepting our offer.

While Jenn and I searched for just the right therapist, we let Buck choose the hands who would eventually work for him. In a surprise move, he hired Jacob and Jeremiah Whitehawk to be his wranglers. Given that they were both excellent horse-men, and the center had been named in their mother's honor, I thought it was the perfect choice.

CHAPTER THIRTY-NINE

THREE MONTHS LATER

The day had finally arrived, after which Dillon Bishop would be spoken for. I couldn't imagine another woman I'd want doing the speaking. Two perfect strangers that had stumbled upon each other in a thrift store in Dallas, Texas. Two lost souls who found more than each other that day. We'd been through a lot together, good times and bad. All of it, enough to fill a book or three, had led us to this day.

I stood on the altar we'd had built at the edge of the pasture with my best friend, Cooper Hill, who keeps reminding me of the bullet he once took for me and probably will until the day I die. Family and friends watched from rows of folding chairs on both sides of the aisle where my beautiful bride would soon walk.

I looked down at my new boots and buttoned the sport jacket that Jolene helped me pick out. It bore a striking resemblance to the one she tried to coerce me into buying for our high school reunion a couple years back. This time, I was happy to oblige.

Buck was there, waiting for his bride to walk down the same aisle. His brother Billy stood with him. Ol' Buck surprised us all when he showed up in a tuxedo. He said he'd always wanted to wear one, but never had occasion to. The top hat might have been a bit much, but Buck was an old soul. Coop said he looked like Mr. Peanut without the monocle.

My favorite part was when Jenn walked down that aisle toward me. Our eyes met, and I know it sounds corny, but my heart skipped a beat or two. That woman made me happier than a hound dog in a room full of biscuits. Hattie followed, and I could tell by the look on Buck's face that he was feeling the same.

Jenn had suggested we write our own vows. It seemed like a reasonable request until I sat down to do it. Now, I'm no writer, but I reckoned we did a decent job when I heard sniffles from the crowd.

The rain clouds that had been gathering all morning passed us by, and the sun broke through just in time for the kissin' part. I saw it as a symbol of the good things to come for our new family. Fire and rain had been part of my life for as long as I could remember. I used to curse the rain for the trouble it brought, never realizing that it was the rain that put out the fires that had threatened to destroy me and everything I loved. Into every life some rain must fall, for without it nothing grows.

After the ceremony, we moved inside to the new meeting room which had been decorated like a down-home barn dance. We toasted to life and love, and ate some of the best barbecue Colorado had to offer. We filled our plates, then filled the dance floor. Jenn and I taught our Colorado friends the Texas two-step and some country line dancing.

During one of our breaks, we sat at our table and watched the action as we caught our breath.

"I have something for you," Jenn said.

I frowned. "I didn't know we were exchanging gifts."

"We're not. Think of it as an investment in our future."

She reached under the table and handed me a flat box with a bow on top. "Open it."

I didn't get presents very often. I shook the box, a habit from my childhood. Something rolled around inside. I shook it again.

"Just open it!"

I don't know which one of us was more excited.

I removed the lid. A pen sat atop neatly folded gold tissue paper. I held it up between us with a puzzled look on my face.

"That's not the important part. See what else is in there."

I peeled back the gold paper to find some legal-looking documents. I scanned the first page. "Adoption papers? You're making it legal?"

"No."

I looked up at her, and our eyes met.

"*We're* making it legal."

I tried to speak, but my heart jumped up into the back of my throat.

"I had Mort draw up the papers. Y'all just have to sign them with that pen in your hand."

I glanced at the pen, then at my new bride. I removed the papers and set them on the table in front of me. Jenn flipped a couple of pages and pointed to the signature line. I couldn't sign that paper fast enough.

I dropped the pen and pulled Jenn in for a celebratory kiss.

"When should we tell him?" she asked.

I scanned the room and called out. "ALEX."

*****

We skipped the honeymoon for Alex's sake. We wanted to stay together for the short time we had left in Colorado. There'd be plenty of time for vacations in the years to come.

Tying the knot didn't change much on the outside, but I'm sure Alex would agree that having a permanent family had a life-changing effect on the inside. We grew closer as the weeks passed. We all pitched in to get the riding center off the ground and prepare for our big move to Texas.

The goal was to buy a small ranch somewhere near Bradley where we could keep a few horses and grow some of our own food. Chance and Romeo were coming with us, but not until we settled into our new home.

The Asha Whitehawk Therapeutic Riding Center opened in August with a full staff and a good deal of community support. As soon as we opened our doors, the VA Medical Centers in Aurora and Grand Junction began referring patients. The Colorado Department of Education also reached out for services under the federal Individuals with Disabilities Education Act.

We rented a small trailer to pull behind the Silverado. I flew Coop in to help us pack and to keep me company on the long ride home while Jenn and Alex followed in her Bronco.

We'd made some friends during our time in Colorado, but none as close as Hattie and her family, and of course, our faithful ranch foreman, Buck. They were all family in our eyes, which made saying goodbye a sad affair.

We loaded the last of our belongings and waited for Hattie and Raven to arrive. I had driven up to the sheriff station in Divide the day before to say my goodbyes to Ziggy and Aunt Ruby. Ziggy offered a letter of recommendation if I ever needed it and suggested I keep in touch.

As I checked the oil in our vehicles one last time, Buck approached with his hands behind his back.

"Where's Alex?" he asked.

"He's inside making his final preparations for the trip, if you know what I mean."

Buck nodded.

Alex ran out the front door.

"Did you wash your hands?"

He spun around and ran back inside.

"He'll be out in a minute," I said.

Buck watched me line up the oil dipstick and push it down into the tube. "Did ya check the transmission fluid?"

"Oil, water, transmission fluid, brake fluid, and tires. I reckon she's good to go."

Buck nodded his approval.

Alex ran out the door and down the steps, wiping his hands on his jeans. He pulled up alongside us and gave Buck a curious look. "What do you have behind your back?"

"Nothin' gets past this one, does it?" Buck looked from me to Alex. "I got you a little goin' away present."

Alex's eyes lit up. "For me? Really?"

Buck held one of his hand-carved statues out in front of him. "It's your horse, Romeo. Made it myself, and I want you to have it."

"Wow! Thank you, Uncle Buck."

With the statue in one hand, Alex threw a big hug around Buck's waist.

Buck didn't know what to do. He looked at me, rolled his eyes, and blinked a couple of times like he wasn't trying to hold back the salt water.

When Alex let go, Buck turned to me. "Got somethin' for you, too."

He reached into his pocket and handed me a trinket.

I studied it for a moment. "This is your Wild Bill Hickok Deputy US Marshall Ring."

"With secret compartment." He smiled an out-of-practice smile. "I want you to have it for the next time you get yourself into trouble."

"Thanks, Buck, but I'm done sticking my nose into other people's business."

"We'll see about that." He looked at his feet. "Maybe you'll remember ol' Buck Owens when you look at it."

"I reckon I will."

I held out my hand. When he grabbed it, I pulled him in for one of those man hugs. I thought all the backslapping would keep a tear or two from falling. I was wrong. When the slapping was done, Buck pulled a rag from his pocket and wiped under his nose.

A car came up the drive as Jenn approached from the house carrying two small coolers.

"We better man up. The girls are here."

Buck waved a dismissing hand. "Ahhh."

Jenn handed one of the coolers to Coop. "There's sandwiches and drinks in there for you boys." She deposited the other one in the Bronco.

Hattie and Raven had tears in their eyes by the time they reached us. After we said our goodbyes all around, Hattie called for a group hug. Everyone joined in, including Buck. We lingered there for a few moments.

Coop pulled out his phone. "Let's get a picture before we leave."

He positioned us, then snapped a few pictures.

Jenn promised to visit a couple of times a year to check in on everything. I watched her hug Hattie one last time, then give me the go signal. She climbed into the Bronco, and we were underway.

When we reached the road, Coop looked left and right. "Which way are we going?"

I hooked a thumb out the driver's window. "We're going home, my friend. We're going home."

* * *

Thank you for investing your valuable time in reading my novel. I hope you enjoyed the story.

Please visit **www.davidhomick.com** for more information about me and my books and to sign up for my mailing list using the button at the top of the page. You can write to me through the site if you're so inclined. I'd love to hear from you.

Word of mouth is the most powerful promotion any book can receive. If you enjoyed this book, please tell your friends. A shout-out on your favorite social media sites would be cool, too.

I want you, the reader, to know that your review is very important to me and to others that may be considering buying this book. You can leave an honest review on Amazon. It doesn't have to be long, just a sentence or two. Your comments are greatly appreciated, but a simple star review is also appreciated.

Thank you, and I wish you all the best.

BOOKS BY DAVID HOMICK

Available on Amazon
Time Traveler's Playlist: A Classic Rock Time Travel Adventure
From Time to Time: A Time Travel Romantic Thriller
Karma Dog: Unleashing Redemption
Changing the Station: How One Stray Dog Found Its Purpose
Don't Curse the Rain (Rain Mystery Trilogy Book 1)
Rain Dance (Rain Mystery Trilogy Book 2)
Fire and Rain (Rain Mystery Trilogy Book 3)
Broken Angels
Reason to Live

www.ingramcontent.com/pod-product-compliance
Lightning Source LLC
Chambersburg PA
CBHW031301120726
47906CB00003B/828